"Are Y...
N...

"That isn't the po...
this habit of inviting men out here to...well, to meet me."

To C.J.'s relief, Garrett just smiled. "I take it she's doing a little matchmaking, is she?"

"She's incorrigible! She's convinced I'm never going to meet a man and fall in love on my own." In spite of herself, C.J. had to smile. "It'll probably be easier if we just play along with her. You don't have to worry that I'll...well, take things the wrong way or anything."

He nodded slowly, his gaze holding hers in that disturbing way he had. "So, in other words, I'm safe."

"As houses."

"Too bad."

C.J. blinked. "Excuse me?"

His slow smile could only be called beguiling. "What if I don't want to be safe, C.J.?"

Dear Reader,

Welcome to March! Spring is in the air. The birds are chirping, the bees are buzzing . . . and men and women all over the world are thinking about—love.

Here at Silhouette Desire we take love *very* seriously. We're committed to bringing you six terrific stories all about love each and every month of the year, and this March is no exception.

Let's start with March's *Man of the Month* by Jackie Merritt. It's called *Tennessee Waltz,* and I know you're going to love this story. Next, Naomi Horton returns with *Chastity's Pirate.* (How can you resist a book with a title like this? You just *can't!*) And look for books by Anne Marie Winston, Barbara McCauley, Justine Davis and new-to-Desire Kat Adams.

And in months to come, some of your very favorite authors are coming your way. Look for sensuous romances from the talented pens of Dixie Browning, Lass Small, Cait London, Barbara Boswell . . . just to name a few.

So go wild with Desire, and start thinking about love.

All the best,

Lucia Macro
Senior Editor

NAOMI HORTON

CHASTITY'S PIRATE

SILHOUETTE *Desire*

Published by Silhouette Books New York

America's Publisher of Contemporary Romance

SILHOUETTE BOOKS
300 East 42nd St., New York, N.Y. 10017

CHASTITY'S PIRATE

Copyright © 1993 by Susan Horton

ISBN: 0-373-05769-5

First Silhouette Books printing March 1993

All the characters in this book have no existence outside the imagination of the author and have no relation whatsoever to anyone bearing the same name or names. They are not even distantly inspired by any individual known or unknown to the author, and all incidents are pure invention.

® and ™: Trademarks used with authorization. Trademarks indicated with ® are registered in the United States Patent and Trademark Office, the Canada Trade Mark Office and in other countries.

Printed in the U.S.A.

Books by Naomi Horton

NAOMI HORTON

was born in northern Alberta, where the winters are long and the libraries far apart. ''When I'd run out of books,'' she says, ''I'd simply create my own—entire worlds filled with people, adventure and romance. I guess it's not surprising that I'm still at it!'' An engineering technologist, she presently lives in Nanaimo, British Columbia, with her collection of assorted pets.

To the Victoria Group
(and you know who you are)
for helping me remember
what's important and what isn't
and
for your deliciously warped sense of humor,
your friendship and laughter,
your belief in excellence in all things.
I am blessed with good friends.

Prologue

"There *is* a catch, of course."

Of course. Garrett's smile was a bit grim. There was *always* a catch.

He took a deep breath and shifted the telephone receiver to his other ear, stalling for time as he contemplated his options. Liking none of them. "And that would be?"

Telling himself—again—that he was doing the right thing. That this entire crazy scheme wasn't going to blow up in his face and leave him looking like the complete fool he probably was....

"She must never know what's going on."

Garrett eased his feet off the corner of his desk and sat up slowly, eyes narrowing. "You're not serious."

"I am deadly serious, young man" came the crisp reply. Her voice was that of someone used to giving orders and having them carried out. "As far as my grandniece is concerned, this conversation never took place. Nor did the one last week when I first contacted you with my little proposition.''

"That is going to be damned hard to pull off."

There was a snort of dry laughter from the other end of the line. "Men lie to women all the time, Mr. Jameison. Especially regarding matters of the heart. Women are always falling in love with men who don't love them back, and although I've always considered it a thoroughly despicable practice until now, I can see where it will work to our mutual advantage in this instance." She gave a sly chuckle. "And besides, if I didn't think you were capable of pulling it off, I'd never have contacted you in the first place."

"I'm starting to wish you hadn't," Garrett growled ungraciously.

"Cold feet, Mr. Jameison?" Amusement still floated through the words. "Already?"

"Let's just say I feel a chill in the air, Lady D'Allaird."

"Bertie," she replied amiably. "Everyone just calls me Bertie. And what I want to know, Mr. Jameison, is if you are up to this or not. If not, say the word and I'll never mention it again. You are not the *only* bachelor on my list, you know."

It was funny, but he'd never thought of that angle before—that he might be just one of numerous fish on her line. He found himself wondering idly if he'd been the first she'd contacted with her madcap idea, or the hundred and first. And if there'd been dozens of infinitely wiser men before him who'd turned her down flat.

And decided, suddenly, that he didn't even want to know.

"More," he muttered, rubbing his face wearily with his free hand. "Tell me more."

It could have been a self-satisfied little chuckle or merely a whisper of static he heard on the line. "The deal's simple. You marry my grandniece, C.J., and I give you controlling interest of Parsons Industrial. Which, as I am sure you know, is of considerable financial value."

Only half a billion or so, Garrett thought dryly, if you counted in their overseas operations and the South American mining interests. Chump change. He found himself grinning at his own wit. Albeit a little wildly. "Almost too considerable," he told her evenly. "It makes me wonder what I might be getting into."

She gave a snort. "You don't think I'd be trying to sell you a pig in a poke, do you? Figuratively speaking, of course."

"The thought," Garrett admitted through a grin, "had crossed my mind."

"And you've already checked it—and C.J.—out thoroughly, Mr. Jameison, or you wouldn't be talking to me now."

Garrett's grin widened as he leaned back in the leather swivel chair again and reached up to loosen his tie. "How do you know you can trust me? What's to stop me from marrying C.J. and taking over the company and eventually either divorcing her and getting a hotshot attorney to make sure the company and money stay mine, or simply mistreating her until she divorces me? Seems to me you're taking a hell of a risk."

"You underestimate me, Mr. Jameison." Her laugh was serene. "You have to be more than just a pretty face to marry into this family—and I've done my research. You didn't get where you are today by being stupid. Besides, I know your father. And your grandfather even better. You are a hardheaded businessman, even ruthless at times, but honorable. If you marry C.J., you will treat her with respect and courtesy and perhaps, in time, even with genuine fondness. And I'd rather go to my grave knowing that, knowing she was being cared for and protected, than taking a chance on her falling in love with an unsuitable man."

Garrett blew a long breath between his teeth and worked the top button on his shirt free, thinking fast. When she'd first approached him with the idea a couple of weeks ago, he'd almost written her off as the eccentric crackpot most people thought she was. Fabulously wealthy and unabashedly flamboyant, she was the youngest daughter of internationally acclaimed industrialist, Augustus Parsons.

She was more than seventy now, but tales of her exploits still reverberated throughout the aristocracy on three continents. She'd been married either four or five times, depending on who you listened to, had consorted with princes, counts, presidents and even the occasional king, and had cut a swath through the grand salons and—so rumor had it—even the bedrooms of Europe and North America with a zest and flare that was still spoken of with awed reverence.

Now she lived on the family estate on the appropriately named Paradise Island just off the gulf coast, and for the past few years had turned her more than capable hand to writing a series of steamy historical novels that had made her one of the top-selling authors in the country.

"I know what you're thinking," she said very suddenly into his left ear. "You're thinking I'm a crazy old woman who's gotten reality confused with the plot from one of her own books."

It was so close to what he *had* been thinking that Garrett held the receiver away from his ear and gave it a suspicious look.

"Actually, it does have possibilities...." She sounded suddenly distracted.

Garrett cleared his throat.

"Sorry, I got a little sidetracked. One of the hazards of old age and an overly active imagination. Where the hell was I...oh, yes. C.J. You were going to ask me a question, I think."

Garrett smiled. "Why the subterfuge? If you want C.J. safely married, why not just introduce her to a handful of eligible bachelors and let nature take its course?"

"Because nature," she replied tartly, "is taking too damned long."

He thought about it for a moment, wondering what else she had up her sleeve.

"Heaven knows," she added with what sounded like a sigh of exasperation, "I've tried! I've dragged a veritable brigade of eminently suitable young men through here, to no avail. My grandniece is a . . . romantic." She made the word sound like a fatal affliction. "She has this dreamy, starry-eyed fantasy of what marriage and love is all about. The problem, of course, is that she has no idea of what she wants. None at all."

"And you do."

"Of course." She sounded surprised he even had to ask. "The man she is looking for, Mr. Jameison, is you."

"She's never met me."

"Trust me, you are everything any young woman would want in a husband. In fact, were I a good deal younger, I'd give you a run for your money myself."

"I doubt," he said dryly, "that I could keep up with you."

She gave a salacious chuckle. "Perhaps not, but you'd enjoy trying."

"And I don't doubt that, either."

"Besides," she said with sudden slyness, "it's time you were married. Oh, I know your reputation—you're quite the ladies' man, always with this beauty or that on your arm. You're a world-league catch, but you always seem to stay one step ahead of the preacher. I'm not too certain why that is, although I have my suspicions it has something to do with your father. But, as it's really none of my business, we won't go into it."

Garrett's fingers tightened around the receiver and he had to force himself to relax.

"The point, however, is that you are nearing that age when men start contemplating their mortality. They start thinking about marriage if they are single, and divorce if they aren't. They begin worrying about their receding hairlines, cholesterol and those extra few pounds they can't seem to shake, about their fading youth and fading dreams. And they start thinking about heirs, Mr. Jameison. About leaving their mark on this earth in some tangible way." She gave a dry chuckle. "Tell me if I'm wrong."

In spite of himself—and the unnerving accuracy of her well-aimed insights—Garrett had to laugh. "You know damned well you're not wrong."

"I won't bore you with my speculations of why you don't believe in love—I'm sure you're as aware of your own weaknesses as the next man. What is important is that you want the security of marriage, and I want my grandniece safely married. The match, as they say, is made in heaven."

"And this 'catch' you mentioned," he reminded her dryly. "What happens if she finds out what we're up to?"

"She won't hear it from *me*" came the baleful reply.

She managed to make it sound like a threat without even trying, and Garrett winced slightly. "And you really think it'll work."

"It has to work, Mr. Jameison." Her voice was softer suddenly. Almost wistful. "I'm not the ogre you must think I am, you know. I love my grandniece more than anything in this world and would do anything to protect her. But I'm getting old. In fact, I may be dying."

She said it with some annoyance, as though the depredations of old age were more an irritation than something to be feared. "I took C.J. in when her parents were killed and raised her like my own. She grew up here on Paradise Island, isolated and innocent and untouched in a little world of our own making. I can see now that it was probably a mistake to keep her so protected from the realities of life. It was an indulgence—well-intentioned, but one I now regret. I can't do anything about that now, but I *can* make certain that she is well cared for when I die. It's that simple."

Simple? Garrett nearly laughed aloud. The whole damned scheme was about the farthest thing from *simple* that he'd heard in years. Corporate mergers were simple. Company takeouts and buyouts were simple. This was *not* simple.

"I want her to be in love, Mr. Jameison. I want that much for her, anyway. And to believe—deeply and completely—that you love her as devotedly. It's all I'm asking, really—that you woo her and win her. Not that it will be difficult. As I said, she's a dreamer and a romantic, and a man of your charm and experience shouldn't have any difficulty in sweeping her off her feet."

"You make it sound easy." Suspiciously easy, he added silently. *Too* easy.

She laughed, a merry sound that tinkled across the miles. "Oh, I never said it was going to be *easy*, Mr. Jameison. I suspect you're going to find that C.J. is quite different from the women you're used to. Quite different, indeed."

Which was not, Garrett decided thoughtfully, exactly the kind of assurance he'd been hoping for. "Different" covered a lot of ground....

"We'll see you on Friday," Bertie was saying cheerfully. "Someone will meet your plane when you arrive in Fort Myers. I presume you know that Paradise is privately owned, with access strictly controlled—the only way on or off the island is by private motor launch."

"Yes," Garrett replied with less than complete enthusiasm. That thought had occurred to him a number of times during their discussion, as a matter of fact—that he was going to be trapped on Paradise with Bertie Parsons D'Allaird and her mysterious grandniece for as long as Bertie wanted it that way.

The receiver at the other end went down with a click and he sighed, dropping his own into its cradle. He gazed out the window of his office and across the metropolitan sprawl of downtown Miami to where land met sea in a tangle of sand, water and beachfront high rises. There was still time to back out. All it would take was a single phone call, and Bertie would toss him back and recast her hook for more daring game.

Or he could just go through with it and consider himself lucky. An arranged marriage was no riskier than marrying for what you thought was love...and what usually turned out to be a whole lot of other things, all of them dangerous as hell and none of them even remotely romantic.

Besides, what did he have to lose? C.J. Carruthers was just a normal, modern, everyday kind of woman, not a real-life version of the beautiful and dangerous Chastity O'Roarke, the hot-tempered, gun-toting heroine of her great-aunt's historical romances. So...how bad could it be, right?

One

The arrow thudded into the palm tree an inch from Garrett's left ear with an evil, vibrating twang.

He was flat on his belly before the slender shaft above him had even stopped humming, mind reeling with stunned disbelief, heart hammering. Not an arrow, some tiny rational part of him said calmly, a bolt from a crossbow. And even more deadly in skilled hands than an ordinary bow.

Not even breathing, he strained to hear something that might give him a clue as to what the hell was going on. But there was nothing, no stealthy rustle of footsteps through grass, no snick of the bow's lever action as another bolt loaded . . . just the undisturbed buzzing of insects in the torpid, late-day heat and, far off, the whoop of a heron.

He swore breathlessly, easing himself to his feet and sliding into the shadows. It was a mistake, he told himself very calmly. Just a random shot loosed into the undergrowth with no intent behind it but carelessness.

Sure, he'd made a few enemies over the years. What good businessman didn't? Hell, there'd even been a time or two when someone had faced him over a board table and had sworn to make him pay. But the thought that one of those disgruntled, even angry, business opponents had actually followed him down here and was stalking him . . .

No. He gave a snort. Odds were that whoever had shot at him was already gone, blissfully unaware of how close he'd come to manslaughter.

But, even knowing that, he decided to stay where he was for a few more minutes. The sun-dappled clump of greenery gave him good cover, and there was no point in being reckless. It *could* have been accidental, but there was also the possibility that he'd stumbled into the middle of someone's drug operation. These little islands dotted up and down Florida's gulf coast were perfect drop points for contraband coming in from Mexico and the Caribbean.

Two minutes passed. Three. Garrett frowned, shrugging his shoulders to loosen taut muscles, and swore impatiently under his breath. If you're out there, he told his invisible assailant, then *do* something, damn it.

Dense with the cloying scent of swamp and moist earth and tropical greenery, the air itself seemed too heavy to sustain even a breath of wind, and the heat wrapped around him like a wet wool blanket. A trickle of sweat made its way down his spine and he shrugged his shoulders again, shaking his head to discourage a cloud of gnats that were zeroing in on him.

That was it. Swearing enthusiastically, he stepped out of his hiding place cautiously, then turned and headed back to the house. Exploring Paradise could wait a day or two; he needed a drink!

He was nearly on his assailant before he even realized it. In fact, if he hadn't paused in the clearing to get his bearings, he would have stepped directly into the man's line of fire. He froze, staring at the figure standing beside the peeling red trunk of a giant gumbo-limbo tree at the edge of the beach.

It was just a boy. Slender, not too tall, a mop of tousled black hair curling damply around his face and neck, he was dressed in ragged jeans and an oversize shirt that hung midway down his thighs. Probably a poacher, Garrett decided. Or some kid from Fort Myers with trouble on his mind.

The boy took a few steps toward the beach, paused indecisively, then turned and walked back to where he'd been standing. He looked nervous, Garrett decided. Almost... scared.

As he damned well should be, Garrett assured himself malevolently as he started to circle. Whoever he was, he could do with a lesson or two in manners.

It took him only a few minutes to work his way around the clearing. The kid was so intent on watching the beach that he didn't hear Garrett coming up behind him until it was too late.

He glanced around at the very last instant and gave a gasp of shock when he saw Garrett towering over him. "How d-did you...?" he managed to stutter. "Y-you were—"

"Dead?" Garrett offered pleasantly. He smiled and reached for the boy with one large hand. "You shouldn't start things you can't finish, kid."

The boy wrenched back and swung the heavy crossbow up and around, and Garrett threw his arm up to block the blow, only half-successfully. The cross arm smacked him on the temple and he gave a growl of pain and anger, swearing as the boy tried to duck under his raised arm and bolt for safety.

"Not on your life, kid!" Garrett lunged forward and caught a fistful of cotton shirt, nearly wrenching the boy off his feet.

The boy gave a yelp of unchildlike profanity and wheeled around with a kick at Garrett's kneecap that would have crippled him had it connected. A sneaker-clad foot thudded into his thigh and he gave a grunt as he grabbed the boy's arm, then in the next instant the kid twisted free with the dexterity of a weasel.

Garrett managed to catch him with one outflung arm. And sucked in a startled breath as his hand closed around the unmistakable fullness of a woman's breast.

He snatched his hand back with an oath, almost giving his captive the break she needed. Giving an eel-like wriggle, she slipped through his grasp like smoke, and for an instant he thought he'd lost her. But his fingers closed around her narrow wrist almost of their own accord and in the next heartbeat he had her again, ignoring thirty-odd years' worth of male indoctrination against hanging on to a woman who didn't want to be hung on to.

But the last of his inhibitions about using physical force vanished as she tried to jackknife her knee into his groin. Swearing, he finally just grabbed a fistful of her hair in one hand, a wad of shirt in the other, and scythed his leg around to sweep her feet out from under her.

They went down together, off balance and struggling, and landed heavily in a tangle of arms and legs and breathless curses. Garrett's captive gave a growl of fury and tried to scramble away on all fours, but he grabbed the waistband of her jeans and slammed her back down. She squeaked as the breath was knocked out of her, but it only slowed her down for the briefest instant and then she was fighting in earnest, rolling onto her back, teeth bared, eyes narrowed and blazing.

"Damn it all, lady, cut it out!" Garrett reared back as her nails slashed the air a millimeter from his face, and he grabbed her windmilling hands.

"Who the hell do you think you are, sneaking up and grabbing me like that!" Her fury seemed to momentarily outweigh her fear and she erupted into a frenzy of clawing fingernails and unnervingly accurate knees.

Taken by surprise, Garrett very nearly lost her. Her fist hit him squarely across the bridge of his nose and he swore and wrenched back, then he caught her by the shoulders as she tried to slither away. Throwing his leg across her to keep her from rolling away, he knelt astride her, knees rammed tightly against her ribs to hold her still, hands grasping each of her wrists.

She wriggled and swore, arching her back to throw him off and trying to bite him. But Garrett simply held her firmly and waited for her to realize she was fighting a losing battle.

To her credit, it didn't take long. Winded, she finally relaxed against the damp ground and glared at him through a tangle of hair. "Damn you," she panted, chest heaving. "I'll have you arrested for this!"

"You'll have *me* arrested?"

She had the most incredible eyes Garrett had ever seen, so deeply blue they were almost violet, and upturned very slightly at the outer corners like a cat's. Her skin was creamy and as smooth as porcelain, tanned to the palest gold, and the tangled hair haloing her face was such a glossy, rich brown it was almost black.

"Who are you?" he growled. "Why were you shooting at me?"

"I live here." She enunciated each word with precision, her eyes snapping like blue witch fire. "And you are trespassing."

She glowered up at him pugnaciously, seemingly forgetting that she was flat on her back on a mostly deserted island, pinned under a complete stranger who had the advantage not only of position but of about eight inches of height and sixty or so pounds of muscle.

She was, Garrett found himself thinking with grudging admiration, nothing if not spunky as hell. And then, as her words started to make some sense, an unhappy suspicion started to take vague shape. "I asked you who you are."

She gave a furious wriggle, tossing her hair out of her eyes. "Get *off* me! I'll give you exactly five minutes to get off this island or I'll take that crossbow and—"

"*That* crossbow?" Garrett asked reasonably, nodding toward the weapon. It was lying where it had fallen when he'd ambushed her, a good ten feet away.

She flushed, as though only now realizing that she was in no position to be offering ultimatums. But she didn't look even half as cowed as Garrett would have liked. In fact, she looked a little *too* thoughtful, as though calculating how to do him the most bodily harm in the least elapsed time.

Not liking the glitter in those impossibly blue eyes, he tightened his grip on her wrists warningly. His suspicions about her identity were becoming stronger by the passing minute, but part of him steadfastly refused to even contemplate the possibility. He found himself desperately hoping that she was just part of Bertie's staff. Or perhaps another guest. Or—

"Let me up or I swear you'll spend the rest of your life in jail!"

C.J. glared up into the coolly handsome face poised over hers. It could have been Jamie Kildonan come to life, she thought inanely. Like the outlaw hero of her great-aunt's historical romance novels, his face was like chiseled stone, and those eyes, so pale a brown they were almost amber, burned with a savage intensity....

Except Jamie was imaginary, and this man, so tall and wide shouldered and cat quick, was very, very real. And, for the first time since he'd stepped out of the shadow and wind whisper to ambush her, C.J. was suddenly afraid.

Screaming wouldn't help. Even if she managed to get out one good yell before he clamped a hand over her mouth, who would come to her rescue? Winthrup? Bertie? Her attacker was built like an athlete, radiating an animal-like vigor and guile that was no match for her seventy-six-year-old great-aunt *or* her equally senior man about the house.

Bluff, she told herself calmly. She was going to have to bluff her way free. "You're in serious trouble," she informed her captor airily, pretending that her situation was completely beneath her notice. "This island is private property and has state-of-the-art security. It's linked directly to the mainland—the police launch would have left Fort Myers almost the instant you set foot on the beach. They'll be here any minute, so I'd really suggest that you—"

"You're lying, Slick," he said calmly. "Try again."

C.J. glowered up at him, sizing up her chances of knocking him off balance and getting away before he could scramble to his feet. Not good, she decided. Besides, even if she did get away from him, she didn't have a hope of outrunning him all the way to the estate grounds. He was too fast and too strong, and he'd have her down before she got fifty feet.

What would Chastity O'Roarke do in a situation like this?

Seduce him, she realized with a sinking heart. Lift her mouth to his and kiss him slowly and deeply, moving that lush, voluptuous body against his to drive him wild and send his senses spinning...and when his defenses were down and he released her wrists to fumble with the lacing of her bodice, she'd snatch his knife from his belt and stab him in the heart....

Except, C.J. reminded herself despairingly, this wasn't 1670. She didn't have any lacing on her bodice—or anywhere else, for that matter—to occupy him. She didn't have a lush, voluptuous body. She wasn't really any too clear on how to administer one of those slow, deep kisses that Chastity was always using to drive her men to distraction. And even if by some miracle she could rattle his composure long enough to get her hand free, he didn't *have* a knife....

"I know kung fu," she sputtered frantically, resorting to 1990s tactics instead. "I have a black belt in—"

"You're still lying." He said it in an offhand manner she found offensively cavalier. "I asked you what your name is."

C.J. made another futile attempt to wriggle out from under him and his eyes narrowed. The muscles in his inner thighs tightened and he shifted slightly, centering his weight over her.

A smile played around one corner of his mouth. "Let's get something straight, Slick—it's not that having you wriggling around like that isn't enjoyable, and I'm not saying you won't get the reaction you're after, but I *can* tell you it's not going to do you a damned bit of good. I've been called a cold-blooded, unromantic bastard on more than one occasion, but even I prefer a *little* foreplay. So stop trying to distract me and just tell me who the hell you are and what you're doing out here."

C.J. went rigid with outrage, feeling a hot blush pour across her cheeks. Glaring at him with all the haughty dignity she could muster, she fought to ignore the outrageously intimate way he was straddling her. "My name," she said with icy precision, "is C.J. Carruthers. I am Colonel Augustus Parsons's great-granddaughter and Lady Roberta Parsons D'Allaird's grandniece, and if you don't take your miserable hands off me this *instant*, you are going to spend the rest of your eternal life in jail!"

She had to stop to catch her breath, realizing to her annoyance that her threat hadn't had any noticeable effect on her captor whatsoever, beyond making his expression darken even more ominously. He didn't look particularly surprised to discover who he had pinned to the ground, but he didn't look especially happy about it.

"C.J. . . . Carruthers." There was a hint of despair in his voice.

She snatched at the possible advantage gamely. "That's right. Now let me up before I have you arrested and—"

"You're hell-bent on having me arrested for something, aren't you?" He gave his head a slow shake and gazed down at her with what could only be called unenthusiastic appraisal. "Well, I'll be damned."

He made it sound more like biblical retribution than an idle curse, and his expression turned a little more bleak.

Then, without warning, he released her wrists and stood up. C.J. rolled away from him and onto her feet, glaring at him from a safe distance.

"Twenty minutes," she said as she started to back toward the beach. "If you're not off the island in twenty minutes, I'll have security turn the dogs loose."

Then soft, hot sand was under her feet, and in the next instant she was sprinting up the beach like a deer, half-drunk with that sheer, insane exhilaration that comes from escaping certain catastrophe.

And behind her, still standing in the shadowed coolness under the trees, Garrett watched the slim figure race up the wide, hot beach with a sense of almost fatalistic doom.

Nothing had prepared him for this. Not even in his wildest dreams had he figured it was going to be *this* bad.

"We had an intruder this afternoon." C.J. frowned at the jeweled comb she had just fixed in Bertie's silver hair. Her great-aunt had given her head a toss at an inopportune moment and the comb had wound up at an odd angle, leaning a little drunkenly to one side. It added a rakish touch that C.J. somehow found fitting, so she nodded and left it.

"Intruder?" Bertie angled the ornate silver hand mirror she was holding to capture C.J.'s reflection and gave her a sharp look. "What kind of an intruder?"

"I didn't waste time making conversation, I just ran him off. He looked like he could have been another real estate agent."

Bertie muttered something mildly scatological. "You'd think they'd have given up by now. I threatened that last lot with buckshot if they ever came around again."

C.J. had to smile. "They all figure you can't live forever."

"Want to bet?"

"Nope." C.J. laughed and gave the second comb a final adjustment. "These are a bit . . . bright, aren't they?"

"What's wrong with 'em?" Bertie turned her head this way and that to better view the glittering combs lifting from her hair like roosters' tails. "Look all right to me."

"Well, don't you think they're a little . . . elegant?"

"Gaudy, you mean." Bertie reached up to pat one of them fondly. "You don't see emeralds that size anymore. And of course they're gaudy . . . vulgar, even. But at *my* age, my girl, a woman has a right to be as vulgar as she wants. If only to simply prove she's still *breathing!*"

"I doubt there's a chance of anyone thinking otherwise," C.J. said dryly. She stepped back and gave an approving nod as she looked Bertie over from head to foot. "Well, you're wearing enough jewelry to founder a horse, that dress is outrageous and—" not even missing a beat, she reached out and took the slender cigarette from Bertie's fingers "—you've got whiskey on your breath. Our guests will be speechless with wonderment."

"And so they should." Bertie looked at her reflection, frowning. She gave the bead-encrusted bodice of her gown an impatient tug, then started lifting and rearranging it experimentally. "There was once a time when grown men wept for a glimpse of these bosoms," she said with disgust. "Now they don't even hold this dress up!" She turned her profile to the mirror. "What do you think about a little lift and tuck?"

"Suggest it to Doc Willerson at dinner tonight. I'm sure he'll be delighted at the prospect of doing breast augmentation on a seventy-six-year-old woman. He'll write you up in the *New England Journal of Medicine,* and if you're lucky, Barbara Walters will call for an interview. Maybe,'' C.J. added, ''they'll even want pictures. That should knock your book sales up another few million—World Famous Author Bares New Breasts. Maybe they'll even ask you to pose for your own covers.''

''You're too clever by half sometimes,'' Bertie said darkly. ''And what did you do with my heart medicine? The glass was sitting right here a minute ago.''

''You mean that glass of whiskey?''

''Heart medicine,'' Bertie repeated serenely.

''Dewars, you mean. Neat.''

''Fine thing when a woman can't even have a drink in her own house.'' Bertie gave her recalcitrant bodice a final tug. ''You'll be locking me in my bedroom next.''

''Don't give me ideas,'' C.J. replied mildly. ''Do you want the black silk wrap, or the red one with the garish embroidery?''

''Garish,'' Bertie snapped with satisfaction. ''You can bury me in the black one. Or, on second thought, keep the black one for yourself and bury me in that beaded job what's-his-name sent me from Italy. I'm sure *you'll* never have a use for it.''

''Oh, I don't know. Once you've gone on to your just reward, I'm planning a series of mad affairs to celebrate.''

Bertie gave a snort. ''You and Winthrup will probably sell off everything I own and bury me naked.''

''Actually, we've decided that when the time comes we'll just wrap you up in an old bed sheet and store you in the attic to save the expense of a funeral altogether. We'll tell people you wandered off one day and never came back.''

''You're a wicked child,'' Bertie said with a sigh. ''I don't know why I ever took you in.''

''Because you love me.'' C.J. gave Bertie's shoulders a fierce hug and grinned at her great-aunt's reflection in the mirror. "Besides, no one else would put up with you. Now finish your face and then we can go down for supper."

Bertie gave C.J.'s hand a pat, then waved her off impatiently and leaned forward in her wheelchair to examine the array of lipstick that C.J. had set out for her. "Red, I should think. Bright red . . . this one." She picked up the gold tube and uncapped it, nodding with approval at the color. Leaning toward the mirror, she started applying it liberally. "Well?" She sat back to admire her handiwork. "How's that? Bright enough?"

"Just about. We'll pass out the sunglasses with the hors d'oeuvres. Ready to go down?"

"Well, I am." Bertie deftly spun the chair around to look at C.J. "But you're not wearing *that,* certainly?"

"And what is wrong with this?" C.J. looked down at her casual linen skirt and silk blouse. In honor of the fact that they were having guests for dinner, she'd hung a handful of gold chains around her neck and had even added the big gold knot earrings Bertie had given her for Christmas.

Bertie's eyebrows lifted. "My dear, that getup may be fine for working in your office or dealing with the tradesmen, but it is entirely unsuitable for entertaining dinner guests."

"Which is fine, as I'm not entertaining anyone. Dr. Willerson is practically family, and this other man is—by your own admission—some poor unsuspecting businessman you're trying to talk into working for Parsons Industrial. I could turn up at the table in sackcloth and neither of them would notice."

"This 'poor unsuspecting businessman' is one of the wealthiest, most influential men in the country. And I'm not trying to talk him into working for PI, I'm offering him the opportunity of a lifetime. And he *will* notice, my dear. Trust me."

C.J. gave Bertie a sharp look. "What are you up to?"

"Up to?" Bertie placed a graceful, bejeweled hand on her chest and gave C.J. a wide-eyed look of spectacular innocence.

"If you're pulling one of your matchmaking stunts again, I swear I *will* lock you in your bedroom!"

"Children! Feed them and house them, and the minute your back is turned they're at your throat."

"Don't mix your metaphors, Aunt Bertie. And if I find out that you lured that poor man out here with promises of a fabulous business proposition just to get your hooks into him, I'll—"

"Well, for heaven's sake! You'd think I spent all my time trying to find you a husband, the way you're carrying on!"

"You *do* spend all your time trying to find me a husband," C.J. said darkly. "That accountant, for instance, who just *happened* to come visiting last summer—you remember him, don't you? The one who went nuts the minute the sun went down?"

"I hardly think 'nuts' is a valid description," Bertie said with a sniff.

"He stripped naked and ran up and down the beach at two in the morning, howling at the moon. I think that qualifies as nuts."

"So, he was a trifle eccentric. Some people might call *me* eccentric, but—"

"People *do* call you eccentric. And what about the architect . . . Ken or Kyle or whatever. I suppose he was just being 'eccentric' when he tried to pry open the wall safe in your office? I don't recall your being very amused at the time."

"How was I supposed to know the man was a drug addict?" Bertie asked peevishly. "Honestly, if you're going to quibble over every little—"

"And then there was Geoffrey, the football hero who had the personality and mental dexterity of a doorstop. And the portrait painter who turned out to prefer men. And the bank president who had that little problem back in Georgia—a wife and three kids. And Morris, the real estate mogul from Tampa. And—''

"There! There!" Bertie waved her hand triumphantly. "Now *he* was a lovely young man! He was *very* interested in you. Before you churlishly ran him off, anyway. I can still remember the hurt expression on his face as he drove away."

"He wanted to rub honey all over my body and lick it off!"

"We all have our little erotic fantasies," Bertie said almost primly. "Who knows, you might even have enjoyed the—''

"*Fantasies?*" C.J. hissed. "He wanted to—''

"I merely suggest that one should at least give some *thought* to broadening one's horizons before rejecting them out of hand."

"Over my dead body," C.J. growled. "No more matchmaking, Bertie—I mean it! If I catch even a whiff of shenanigans tonight, I'm going to have Willerson declare you incompetent on the spot. I'll sign the committal papers then and there and you'll be in Hillcrest Rest Home by morning."

"You think anyone would accept *Willerson's* medical opinion? The man's a quack!" Bertie gave a derisive snort. "And besides, everyone would know you were just after my money. There are laws protecting helpless old ladies from conniving relatives."

"Helpless, my foot. And if anyone in this family needs protection from conniving relatives, it's me."

"Really, C.J., you are the most suspicious person!"

"I can't imagine why."

"If you're hoping to make me forget that I want you to change for dinner, you're quite mistaken," Bertie put in as though they'd never been talking about anything else. "And I am not up to any 'shenanigans.' I have some complicated business matters to discuss with Mr. Jameison and it's more convenient to do it here than at his offices in Miami, that's all. And although it did not escape my notice that the man is devilishly good-looking, well established *and* eminently eligible, I did not have any ulterior motives for asking him to stay a few days."

"Stay?" C.J.'s eyes narrowed slightly. "Here? At the estate?"

"Well, of course here. Where else would the man stay? In a tent on the beach? I've put him in the Green Cottage."

"Of course you did," C.J. said with amazing self-control. The Green Cottage was right next to her own small bungalow, with nothing but a trellis laden with bougainvillea and a threadbare palm between them.

No ulterior motives? Greeks bringing wooden horses into the walls of the estate would have fewer!

"Now be a darling," Bertie was saying sweetly, "and run and change. That scarlet evening gown with all the beadwork should do nicely. With your grandmother's ruby-and-diamond necklace, of course. And for heaven's sake, do something with your hair! I *can't* understand why anyone with such lovely hair insists on having it chopped off willy-nilly and—"

"Enough, already! I'm going, I'm going!" C.J. held up her hands to quell the flood, not in any mood for one of Bertie's well-intentioned lectures on the art of being fashionable and alluring. Not tonight. She was still shaken from her encounter with the stranger and wanted nothing more than to crawl into bed with a supper tray and a good mystery, preferably with the TV blaring for extra distraction.

But that, obviously, wasn't to be. Bertie was in an "entertaining" mood. And *that* meant all of Paradise Island was expected to cooperate.

There was the usual collection of small, foul-tempered dogs hanging around the doorway, waiting for Bertie to accompany them downstairs where they'd terrorize everyone within ankle-biting range. C.J. skirted them, keeping a sharp eye on the ancient gray poodle-cross that moved in behind her with astonishing speed, given her age and general decrepitude.

"Taffy!"

The old dog looked around at Bertie guiltily, then flashed C.J. a look of pure hatred that C.J. merely returned with a benevolent smile. "One day, dog," she murmured. "It's going to be just you and me and a trip to the pound...."

"What did you say, darling?"

"I said I think there's a rip in my gown. The red one, I mean. I stepped on the hem at the Lakersons' Christmas party and put my heel through it."

"Oh, rats," Bertie said with a hint of irritation. "Then it will have to be that little black knit number I bought for you in New York last month. The one that—"

"—makes me look like a Miami streetwalker."

"Nonsense! You have a beautiful body. It's a sin the way you keep it hidden under all those horrible sweatshirt things."

"Considering that this mysterious Mr. Jameison is here *only* to discuss business," C.J. said, pausing in the doorway to look around, "I can't imagine why it matters."

Bertie waved an elegant hand in airy dismissal. "I was *attempting* to instill a bit of elegance to the proceedings, that's all. Although I don't know why I bother. It's like being incarcerated with the Philistines, living in this house with you and Winthrup. We'd be eating off paper plates and charring things on one of those barbecue gadgets if it were up to you. When one has dinner guests, one should behave—and dress—accordingly."

C.J. simply smiled. "I'll come by in about twenty minutes to take you down. And in many parts of the country, Bertie, eating dinner around a barbecue is considered fine dining."

Bertie shuddered visibly. "Not in this house, young lady. Not while I still draw breath!"

* * *

The two large guest cottages sat about a hundred yards from the main house, tucked in a grove of sea grape and red-barked gumbo-limbo and tall Australian pines. They were screened from the house, and one another, by trellises covered with flaming bougainvillea and a mad riot of climbing roses that filled the damp, warm evening air with their scent.

The western sky was aflame, and Garrett rested his elbows on the stone seawall to watch the swollen sun inch its way toward the horizon. It hung in the sky like a shimmering fireball, streaked with crimson-and-azure clouds and setting the water of the gulf aflame. And then, almost abruptly, it dropped, its fires cooled and finally extinguished. The sky's colors faded to soft pastels, pearlized and crystalline clear and almost more beautiful in their subtlety than the blazing peacock display of only moments before.

It was something he never got used to, that swift transition from day to night. In Wisconsin, where he'd been born and had grown up, summer evenings went on forever.

But here...he shook his head, smiling. One blaze of color, then a heartbeat of dusk, then that thick, velvety tropical night filled with hot scented breezes and the whisper of the sea and a million stars, undimmed until the moon rose hours later.

It was a time of magic and endless possibilities, when—if you believed hard enough—almost anything could happen. And what man was beyond a little wishful thinking...?

Garrett gave himself a slight shake, realizing he'd been staring out across the restless waters of the gulf without seeing a thing. A squadron of pelicans was swinging by, scant inches above the crests of the long, foam-rilled rollers, and a little farther out something with a graceful neck and long, trailing legs flapped its way leisurely northward. The boom and hiss of the breakers piling up on the narrow strip of sand beyond the seawall filled the air and he found himself drifting again.

Thoughtfully he touched the bruise on his temple where C.J. had walloped him with the bow. If this was the way she routinely greeted strangers, it didn't take any great mental dexterity to figure out why the hell she wasn't married—or even close to it. And no greater leap of logic to figure out why Bertie had decided to take matters into her own hands.

Shoving himself away from the seawall, he shrugged his shoulders to settle his dinner jacket across them, then shot his cuffs and adjusted them. And then, eyes narrowed slightly, he started toward the house with long, purposeful strides.

Two

He was met at the door by a slathering pack of pint-size dogs that hurtled across the threshold and down the wide steps as a single unit, claws clattering on the slate tiles, their barks rising hysterically as they made a beeline for him.

A stooped figure appeared in the open doorway behind them. "*Shut up,* you useless lot of—" The rest was lost under startled yelps and the sound of clawed feet scrabbling on tile as the dogs skidded to a confused halt, falling over one another in their haste to get turned around and back through the door. "Go on, go on!" He shook his fist at the dogs as they raced madly by him.

Their excited barks faded in the depths of the huge old house and Winthrup gestured impatiently for Garrett to follow him. "Don't know why she keeps those things. Cats at least earn their keep. I like cats. But those dogs of hers..." He shook his head, muttering things under his breath.

"I heard that!" A voice that Garrett recognized as Bertie's snapped around them. "If anything's useless around here, it's you. Where the *hell* is my drink? I asked you to get it an hour ago."

"Barely three minutes ago, your Ladyship," Winthrup replied serenely as he led Garrett into the vast living room. "Lemonade, was it, or mineral water?"

"*Whiskey,*" the voice roared from the depths of a chair by the fireplace. "Don't you lemonade *me!*"

"No whiskey." Winthrup's smile was only faintly malicious. "Doctor's orders. I'll have Cook make you up a cup of mint tea."

"Tea, my—why, Garrett Jameison, it's so nice to see you." The diminutive figure in the electric wheelchair by the fireplace smiled up at him sweetly and held out a slender ring-bedecked hand. "I'm so glad you could join us."

"I wouldn't have missed it for the world, Lady D'Allaird. You have a way of piquing a man's interest, to put it mildly."

She gave a soft laugh, sharp brown eyes twinkling. "There was once a time, young man, when I could pique a man's interest without blandishments and bribery."

"I have no doubt of that whatsoever."

"And please, let's dispense with this 'Lady' business. I am simply Bertie. My husband has been dead for many, many years. I haven't been a 'Lady' for a long while now."

"And that's the truth," Winthrup murmured. "A drink for the gentleman? Whiskey, perhaps?"

"You're fired, Winthrup," Bertie snapped.

"Yes, your Ladyship," Winthrup said without even blinking. "We have a rather good Scotch," he continued for Garrett's benefit, apparently unperturbed by the fact that he was out of a job. "I'm sure you'd find it quite enjoyable." He turned his head to smile down at Bertie. "And I'll get her Ladyship her tea."

"Don't enjoy yourself too much," Bertie told him with equal charm. "I've cut you out of my will, you know. You were counting on living high on the hog on my money after

I go—don't bother denying it!—but you're not getting a penny." She smiled an evil smile. "Or maybe the dogs, Winthrup, would you like that? I'll put in a proviso that you'll get a stipend as long as they are well cared for."

"Yes, Madam, if you say so." Winthrup gave Garrett a long-suffering smile. "She gets like this now and again." He tapped his temple with his finger, nodding sagely. "The mind, you know. It's always the first to go."

"Not before I see you fired, old man," Bertie said tartly. "Now quit lollygagging around and get my whiskey! And none of that watered-down stuff you serve company, either—the Dewars. And be quick about it!"

Turning away, Winthrup rolled his eyes dramatically heavenward, and Garrett swallowed a smile.

"Sit, sit," Bertie said, waving her hand toward the big wing chair across from her. "I've sent C.J. on a couple of errands to keep her busy for a few minutes so we could talk. You've not met her yet, have you?"

Garrett hesitated. "Not . . . really."

"Good. I want to make certain our deal is still on before we go ahead with dinner. After all, if you're backing out, further discussion is irrelevant."

Garrett had to smile. "You don't beat around the bush, do you?"

"Either you're going to accept my proposition, or you are not." The small dark eyes holding his glittered with impatience. "So do we have a deal?"

Garrett hesitated, eyes narrowed on the woman across from him. She had a small brown simian face and she looked as fragile as crystal. And yet you could see the strength in her, the fierce intelligence, the shrewd understanding of the world and how it worked.

"You think I'm a mad old woman, don't you?"

"I think you're anything but," he said with a snort of laughter. "Which is what scares me."

She gave a merry laugh, those bright brown eyes sparkling like glass beads. "My father started Parsons Industrial from nothing at the turn of the century, and today we hold interests in a multitude of ventures in over twenty countries. But you know all that. You wouldn't be here if you didn't."

"I . . . checked into things after you called."

She smiled. "If you hadn't, I'd have called the whole thing off myself. I do not want my grandniece marrying a stupid man. Or a reckless one."

"You don't call this reckless?"

"I call it a prudent business decision, Mr. Jameison. For both of us."

Garrett nodded slowly, looking at her steadily. "Which brings us to what you—personally—get out of this. Besides peace of mind, I mean. There must be more."

A satisfied smile flickered across her mouth, and Garrett had the feeling he'd just passed some test he hadn't even been aware of.

She simply smiled again. "When my father became too ill to run things, he turned control of PI over to his three children—my brother James got forty-nine percent of the company, and my sister and I received the remaining fifty-one percent jointly. Quite truthfully, neither Clara nor I paid particular attention to the business. We signed whatever James put in front of us, and everything thrived. I ran off and married my darling Frenchman, and Clara married John Carruthers and had two sons, one of whom was C.J.'s father. Are you with me so far?"

"I'm with you."

"Clara died, bequeathing me her share of the fifty-one percent of PI, but, as before, I simply signed what James wanted me to sign and gave him my proxy in any voting matter. After my husband died, I came home. C.J.'s parents had been killed in an accident four years before, and when I got back I discovered two things—one, that C.J. was being handed around the family like a stray kitten no one wanted, and second, I actually *enjoyed* playing business tycoon.''

She grinned. ''Much to everyone's consternation, I started attending board meetings. James and his son and two grandsons were more or less running things by then, and I'd come swooping down on them in my best Parisienne gowns and my hats and my jewels, just to give them a good shaking up. I asked questions. I poked my fingers into things. And, for the most part, I did not like what I heard.''

She frowned a little, hands resting across the carved handle of an elegant walking stick. ''We had money in chemical companies that were poisoning our rivers, and logging companies that were destroying our forests, and munitions companies that were making weapons to slaughter children. We dealt with death, Mr. Jameison. We made bombs. We made deals with governments that intimidated and butchered their own people. We made money, yes—great wads of it. But at great moral cost.''

''So you started becoming more involved.''

''James and the boys hated it at first. But what could they do? I held—hold—controlling interest in the whole damned shebang. It was do as Aunt Bert says, or get out.'' She smiled slyly. ''They're all terrified of me up there in New York. Not that I actually meddle in their affairs personally these days—I'm much too busy with my writing. But my CEO, Emmett Royce, handles everything for me. Or did.'' The smile faded.

''Like me, Emmett is getting old. He's had to retire, dumping PI back into my lap. And frankly, I have better things to do than terrorize my brother's children into running a clean ship.''

''And they see an opportunity to pull off a coup and take control.''

''They're positively salivating at the prospect,'' Bertie said with an evil chuckle. ''They think I'm just a dotty old lady.

And the fact that I write novels makes it even worse. I'm not just dotty, but in very poor taste, to boot.''

She smiled a benign little smile that gave Garrett goose bumps. ''They've grown fat and sassy, tolerating old Aunt Bertie because she's richer than God and won't live forever. With Emmett gone, they think it's almost all theirs. But I intend to fool 'em.'' She gave a cackle of laughter. ''I might not live forever, but I damned well intend to live long enough to see PI in good hands before I go. Your hands, Mr. Jameison. C.J. is my legal heir. Marry her, and that fifty-one percent of the company is yours.''

Garrett tapped his lower lip with his thumbnail, nodding slowly. ''Why not just turn it over to her now?''

''They'd tear her to shreds,'' she said bluntly. ''I'm not a particularly sentimental person, Garrett, but I do not want PI turned into something my father would not be proud of. Does that strike you as silly?''

''It strikes me as a prudent business decision.''

She gave a snort of laughter. Then, smile fading, she pinned him with a steely look. ''Well, Mr. Jameison, what's your answer? Yes, or no?''

Garrett narrowed his eyes slightly, wondering how far he could bluff her. Deciding, even as he was contemplating it, that his chances were about nil. And besides, he asked himself brutally, why not? Everything she'd said was right. He was tired of being one of the country's most eligible bachelors. And love didn't come into it at all.

''You've got yourself a deal,'' he said quietly, holding out his hand. ''I imagine you've got papers you want me to sign.''

She gave a chuckle. ''Indeed I do. I may trust you with my grandniece, and I even trust you with the family business, but not necessarily with *both*. Divorce C.J., or in any way harm her, and you'll forfeit everything. And don't think for a minute you can hornswoggle me. The marriage contract is bulletproof.''

"Done," he said hoarsely, wondering why he suddenly felt so weary.

"That woman is going to drive me to drink," C.J. muttered as she half ran down the sweeping staircase to the elegant, two-story-high entrance hall, juggling an armful of files. "Why she thinks she needs these right now, I don't—Winthrup! Thank heaven *someone's* around. I was beginning to think she'd fired everyone and hadn't bothered to tell me."

"Cook's quit," Winthrup said with a sigh as he waited for her at the bottom of the stairs.

"Again? What's the problem *this* time?"

"Her Ladyship, it seems, knows better than Cook how to prepare beef Wellington."

"I hope you were able to smooth things over."

Winthrup slipped the files out of C.J.'s arms. "For the time being, but things got quite unpleasant for a bit. And while we're discussing household difficulties, Miss C.J., we'll need to advertise for a downstairs maid again. That Chantal person left in a huff an hour ago. Something about an argument over how to set a dinner table."

"That didn't take long. How long was she here—two weeks?"

"Almost." Winthrup smiled over the armful of files, eyes twinkling. "Your aunt sent me to tell you to put a move on. These files, it seems, aren't important, after all."

"I'm going to strangle her one of these days," C.J. said conversationally. "And they won't even put me in jail. In fact, I'll probably get a commendation or something."

"Now, now," Winthrup said disapprovingly. "She's getting on, you know. We all have a right to be difficult when we get on."

"You've been reading her copy of *Creative Aging* again," C.J. said dryly. "There's difficult, Winthrup. And then there's impossible." She started to turn toward the living room, stopped and looked around. "Dr. Willerson's been here a lot lately. Is something going on with Bertie's health that I don't know about?"

He pursed his mouth thoughtfully. "Not that I'm aware of, Miss. The doctor was here for dinner last week, of course, but..." He shrugged, his expression of disapproval deepening. "He comes for dinner every week. I sometimes think he has mistaken us for a restaurant."

C.J. had to swallow a smile. "He's sweet on her, Winthrup, you know that."

Winthrup gave a sniff. "Fat lot of good it will do him."

"Well, you and I know that, but Willerson lives on in hope. Personally I think it's great—the more time he spends here, the sharper the eye he keeps on Bertie."

That precipitated another snort. "*Too* sharp, if you ask me."

"So all these extra visits of Willerson's are simple wishful thinking and not professional? She's feeling all right...."

"Extra visits, Miss?"

"He was here on Monday night, then again on Wednesday."

The pause, when it came, didn't last even a heartbeat. No one else would have noticed it, C.J. thought with a chill. You wouldn't—unless you'd known him almost forever.

"I think you must be mistaken, Miss. I'm sure that had Dr. Willerson been on the estate, I'd have known." He nodded toward the files in his arms. "I'll take care of these. And you'd better go in there. You know how she gets when she's kept waiting."

C.J. grimaced. "All too well. And...thanks, Winthrup." She watched as he hurried toward Bertie's office, suddenly scared to death. He was lying. For the first time in the twenty-three years she'd lived here, Winthrup had lied to her.

"Oh, God, Bertie, what's wrong?" Her whisper rustled through the shadows around her, and C.J. rubbed her bare arms, trying not to shiver. "What's happening, Bertie? Why aren't you telling me what's happening?"

For some reason, Garrett kept watching the door.

Like a gunslinger in a saloon, he found himself thinking ruefully: one eye on the bartender—and Bertie filled the role admirably—the other scanning the room for a possible ambush.

Not that he expected her to come in shooting or anything. At least, he *doubted* she'd come to dinner armed and dangerous.

Then again, from what he'd seen of C.J. Carruthers so far, anything was possible.

So, reasonable or not, he managed to maneuver both himself and Bertie so his back was to the wall and no one could come up behind him.

And yet, even expecting her, he was still caught by surprise when she did finally step through the doorway.

For one thing, she just sort of materialized—one moment the doorway was empty, and the next she was just *there*. Bertie had just spun her wheelchair deftly toward the generously stocked liquor tray, and it was she that C.J. saw first. Unnoticed, he stood in the shadows near the fireplace and watched curiously as she walked toward Bertie with a wide smile.

It took him a moment or two to convince himself that it *was* C.J. he was looking at. The C.J. who had ambushed him in the mangrove swamp not an hour earlier; the C.J. who had come within a gnat's whisker of skewering him to a palm tree with that damned crossbow.

That C.J. had been little more than a girl, short black hair all atangle and falling in her eyes, expression pugnacious as any tomboy's, face smudged with dirt and sweat. But *this* C.J. . . . .

Garrett whistled silently between his teeth, his spirits taking a decidedly upward turn. This, he decided with suddenly renewed interest, was more like it!

She seemed taller, for one thing, although that was probably on account of the expensive bronze-and-gold evening sandals . . . not to mention the truly breathtaking length of leg above them. The dress was simple and black, no more than an artful swatch of fabric that ended at mid-thigh and hugged her slender body in a way that could only be called interesting.

She was wearing a pair of big bronze-and-copper earrings that swung when she turned her head, and a loose belt of intertwined ropes of tiny jet-and-bronze beads that glittered like liquid fire as she walked, emphasizing the subtle sway of her body.

Bertie said something that made her laugh, and Garrett found himself staring at her, thinking shrewdly—maybe a little too shrewdly—that she'd look good with him. And then remembered, with an odd little twist in his gut, that this wasn't just another good-looking woman who'd be a part of his life for a few weeks or even months. This one was for keeps.

There was a sudden coiling of tension in his belly, but before he had time to figure out if it was anticipation or guilt, she'd looked around, those amazing blue eyes searching the room, and then she was looking straight at him.

It took her a moment. He'd at least had the advantage of knowing who she was; she, on the other hand, simply stared uncomprehendingly at him, a tiny frown marring her forehead as she realized she'd seen him before, should know him from somewhere . . . searched her memory for where and when. . . .

And then, abruptly, her eyes went wide, and even from halfway across the huge room he could see the color drain from her face. He shot her a cool smile and started to stroll slowly, casually, toward her.

"What the *hell* is *he* doing here!"

"What what?" Bertie looked up guiltily.

"I said, what—" C.J. glanced down at her great-aunt, then at the glass in her hand, and swore, the stranger momentarily forgotten. "What on earth do you think you're doing?"

"Willerson said it's good for me," Bertie said defensively. "Just like real medicine, he said."

"He said no such thing."

"He certainly did! You can ask him yourself as soon as he—"

"You have the most selective hearing—and the most creative interpretation of what you *do* hear—of any person I know," C.J. muttered as she took the glass from Bertie's hand, ignoring the thunderous scowl it earned her. "He said that an occasional small glass of spirits wouldn't harm you, he did *not* say it was good for you. And the operative word was *small*." She held up the water tumbler half-filled with Scotch. "There's enough here to provision the entire Atlantic Fleet for winter maneuvers."

"Lord, you can be tedious at times." Bertie gave her shoulders an indignant shrug that nearly unseated the beaded silk shawl across them. "Carrie Nation herself wasn't half the prig you've become lately."

"Carrie Nation didn't have to put up with you," C.J. shot back. "You've got to start taking better care of yourself, Bertie. I know it's fun trying to outwit Winthrup and Willerson and me, but you're the only great-aunt I've got and I've grown kind of fond of you over the past twenty-three years."

"You call the way you treat me *fond?* Heaven help me if you ever start *disliking* me."

"Don't be unpleasant. We've got company, remember?" And it was only then that she lifted her head to look at the tall, tawny-eyed stranger who had wandered across to stand beside them. And wondered, as she did so, which was making her heart pound more: Bertie's recklessness with the bottle of Scotch, or the fact that the man she'd nearly killed that afternoon was none other than her great-aunt's prospective new business partner.

He was staring down at her challengingly, and C.J. somehow held his gaze, knowing that her cheeks were glowing an uncomfortable—and incriminating—shade of pink. "And you, I presume, are Garrett Jameison."

"Well, for heaven's sake, C.J.," Bertie muttered, "you could at least wait for me to introduce you properly. What *has* gotten into you this evening, anyway?" She edged her wheelchair between them, giving C.J. a rap on the ankle that was not, C.J. suspected, entirely accidental. "Garrett, this precipitous young woman, as you've probably gathered, is my grandniece, C.J. Carruthers. She's usually much better mannered than this, but something's set her off. C.J., be nice and say hello."

C.J. looked up at Jameison and honored him with a frosty smile so insincere it hurt her mouth. He was doing it on purpose, of course—standing so close she had to bend her head right back to meet his eyes. He was obviously one of those men who deliberately used his height—and the not-inconsiderable breadth of those well-tailored shoulders—to intimidate anyone he thought worth intimidating.

"I presume you've told my great-aunt all about our escapade this afternoon."

"Escapade?" Bertie's head shot around. "What escapade?"

Jameison smiled. "Actually, I hadn't."

Bertie was drawing in a breath for a barrage of questions and C.J. gritted her teeth. "We—"

"I was exploring the island this afternoon when your grandniece spotted me," Jameison said easily, his gaze amused and lazy. "She figured I was trespassing and…ran me off."

"She did *what*?" Bertie gave C.J. a scandalized look. "*This* is the man you thought was a real estate agent?"

"If you'd bothered to tell me that you'd invited Jameison as a houseguest," C.J. said defensively, "it wouldn't have happened. But when I saw him sneaking around, I—"

"And if you'd stop trying to protect me, young lady, we wouldn't even be having this conversation." Bertie looked at her sternly. "If he *had* been an intruder, you could have been hurt, C.J.. You lecture me about taking care of myself and I find you're out running around playing Green Beret!"

"If it's any consolation," Jameison drawled, "she knows how to take care of herself in a tight spot."

Bertie gave C.J. a steely look. "Well, I don't want to hear about your getting into any more 'tight' spots, young lady. You're all the family I have, except for Bertram and his clan, and I've invested too much time and energy into raising you to see you murdered at the hands of some scalawag. Tomorrow we're looking into getting permanent security guards out here. *They* can roam the beaches watching for intruders, and you, my girl, can stick to taking care of *me*."

"How about a trade?" C.J. smiled at Bertie, trying to jolly her into a smile. "Armed intruders aren't half the challenge you are on a good day."

"And don't think flattery will get you off the hook. I'm most distressed, C.J. *Most* distressed. Give me that." She reached for the glass of Scotch. "I feel positively *wan*."

C.J. stepped across to put the glass safely out of reach on the mantel. "You've never been wan a day in your life. And besides, I thought Mr. Jameison was here to discuss business. Another shot or two of Dewars under your belt, and he'll walk off with the company."

"Ignore her, Garrett," Bertie said airily. "*We* all do. She's been on a temperance crusade all week. Last week it was tobacco. Next week it'll probably be sex."

"Bert!" C.J. was infuriated to feel another blush glaze her cheeks. "*Would* you act your age!"

"I am," Bertie said serenely. "I might be a little slower than I was fifty years ago, but no less able to enjoy a good—"

"*Bert!*"

"I see you decided to take my advice about what to wear tonight."

"I thought you'd approve," C.J. said testily, starting to feel slightly harried. It wasn't Bertie—she wasn't behaving any differently than she did most days—but the way Jameison kept watching her, his gaze hooded and lazy and just a bit too thorough. "I look like a—"

"—completely normal, attractive young woman...a vast improvement over that tomboy gear you usually wear." Bertie ran an assessing eye over the dress. "Mind you, if I still had legs like yours I'd hike that hem up another inch or two."

"Hike the hem up another inch or two and there'll be a lot more Carruthers real estate on display than just leg." There was no point in getting annoyed with Bert, C.J. knew. She'd worn the dress on a complete whim, deciding to let Bertie win this argument just once—only to regret it the instant she'd set eyes on Jameison.

Or, more correctly, the instant he'd set eyes on her.

"Don't be vulgar, dear," Bertie said primly.

"Madam," a sonorous voice broke in from behind them, "dinner will be served in five minutes."

"And not a *moment* too soon. People have starved to death in less time than it takes to get a meal put on the table in this house! And where is Willerson? He should have been here an hour ago." She spun her chair around with surprising strength for someone who was half-starved. "*Winthrup!*"

"Madam?"

"Call that quack and tell him the invitation's off. If he can't—"

"Dr. Willerson has just arrived, Madam," Winthrup said in his very best man-about-the-house manner, seemingly inspired to new heights of civility—if not servility—by Jameison's presence. "He will be joining you in a moment."

"C.J., darling," Bertie said suddenly, "would you run and fetch my walking stick from my office? And take Garrett with you. You can show him where all the PI files are kept."

"Bert, this is hardly the time for a guided—" C.J. snapped her mouth closed at Bertie's sharp look. She narrowed her eyes slightly. "If I didn't know better, I'd suspect you were getting rid of me so you could talk with Willerson in private. Which would make me suspect that you have a medical problem you don't want me to know about. Which—"

"If I had a medical problem," Bertie said tartly, "the last person I'd call would be a quack like Willerson. I just want you to show Garrett the office, is that asking too much?"

"No." C.J. swallowed the fear rising in her throat, wondering why she'd never noticed how frail Bertie looked. Surely she hadn't been that pale yesterday. And had the tremor in her hands always been so pronounced?

"Well?" Bertie's voice snapped her out of her brooding. "Get on with it, girl!"

There wasn't a lot she could do but go. And, fuming silently, C.J. did just that. She stalked out of the room without even so much as a glance in Jameison's direction. If he wanted to go with her, fine. If he didn't, that was his problem. This was as good a time as any for him to learn that one did not defy the gorgon in her own lair.

To her annoyance, he seemed no more inclined to argue with Bertie than she was and a moment later he fell into step beside her. "Your great-aunt is quite a woman."

"She's not well. I don't want you upsetting her."

"She looks pretty healthy to me."

"Well, she's not." C.J. gave him a hostile look. "I don't know why she's getting involved with Parsons Industrial, anyway. Big business bores her, she's always said that."

"It's her family business. She's the major shareholder."

"Bertie's a writer. She makes her living writing historical novels, not sitting around smoky boardrooms playing CEO. She's never been interested in the company, hasn't gone to a board meeting in years, always signs her proxy over to Emmett Royce. He and my uncle run PI, not Bert."

She was getting more irritated by the minute and didn't even know why. "Just why *are* you here, anyway? I can't imagine what Bertie has that could interest a man like Garrett Jameison. I thought you were only interested in companies you could break up and sell off bit by bit." C.J. stopped dead. "Is PI in financial trouble? Is that why you're here—to convince Bertie to sell you her part of the corporation so you can—"

"Relax," Garrett said with a slow smile. "Your great-aunt figures PI needs some new blood, that's all. She's not sure she likes some of the decisions being made on her behalf, but, as you said, she's not interested in running it herself, either. So she called me and asked if I'd be interested in looking into things." The lazy smile widened. "I like a challenge, so I decided why not."

But that wasn't all of it, C.J. thought coolly, staring up into those pale golden eyes. Not by half. Bertie wouldn't have suddenly gone looking for outside help unless things were a hell of a lot worse than Jameison was letting on. And Garrett Jameison—the man *Time* magazine called the Miami Shark—wouldn't have wasted his time coming all the way out to Paradise unless the pickings promised to be very good, indeed.

Whatever was going on between Bertie and this man, it was big. But the question was, just where did C.J. Carruthers fit in?

"You're not married, are you, Mr. Jameison."

Something may have shifted very slightly in the depths of his eyes, something suddenly wary. "I wish to hell you'd start calling me Garrett. And, no, I'm not. Why?"

C.J. had to smile. "The country's most eligible bachelor, I think *Newsweek* called you."

He winced. "I hope you don't believe everything you read."

"Is it true you've dated the most beautiful women in the country?"

"I read that article, too," he told her with a droll smile. "And I *don't* choose my women on the basis of their breast size."

"Of course you don't," C.J. agreed gently.

He winced again, more theatrically this time. "You're a hard sell, aren't you."

"That depends on what you're trying to peddle."

To her surprise, he threw his head back and laughed, those odd golden eyes glowing slightly in the dim lighting of the corridor. "Just my native charm, Miss Carruthers. Just my charm."

"In which case, Mr. Jameison," she said with a dry smile, "you're going to find me a very hard sell, indeed."

His eyes captured hers, amused and warm, and he seemed suddenly a little taller and wider and closer than he had only a heartbeat before. His mouth still held the remnants of laughter, one corner canted higher than the other. "As I said... I like a challenge."

It wasn't the words themselves that made her heart give a completely unnecessary thump, but the expression on his face as he said them. There was something anticipatory in the way he was looking down at her, almost... predatory.

C.J. suppressed a little shiver and turned away—casually, she hoped—and pushed open the door to Bertie's office. "Why didn't you tell me who you were this afternoon?"

"You didn't give me a chance."

"You didn't make much of an effort." She flicked the desk lamp on and looked around the spacious, well-appointed office for Bertie's walking stick.

"You caught me by surprise. The way Bertie spoke of you, I was expecting someone more..."

"More what?" C.J. gave him a speculative glance.

"Demure." He grinned ingenuously. "Genteel."

C.J. smiled coolly. "I can be as genteel as hell when it suits me, Mr. Jameison. Most days it doesn't."

"You're very protective of her."

C.J. had to smile. "When I'm not threatening to throttle her with my bare hands." Then she paused, her smile fading, and turned to look at him. "I hope that was just an observation and not a question. Because, yes, I *am* very protective of her. And if I thought she was getting into something that would hurt her, I'd be very...upset."

His smile was lazy. "Your great-aunt and I are negotiating a business deal, C.J., that's all. And if it makes you feel better, she's the one with the ace up her sleeve."

She looked at him for a long moment, then nodded, having to smile again. "She usually is. You'll be lucky if you come out of this deal with your shirt."

"Oh, I think I'm going to come out of it with a hell of a lot more than that," he murmured, his gaze seeming to hold hers. "In fact, I'm beginning to think I may have made one of the best deals of my life."

"Really." She didn't like the way he was looking at her, C.J. thought a little desperately. There was something about the way his gaze drifted across her face, feature by feature, that unnerved her, making her feel suddenly awkward and self-conscious. "Can you, um, that walking stick has got to be in here somewhere!"

He just smiled, not saying anything, and C.J. felt the blood rush to her cheeks, wishing she'd said to hell with it two hours ago and had simply stayed in her cottage with a bowl of soup, sanity intact. "And I'd appreciate it if you didn't tell her about this afternoon. She'd misinterpret what happened and get all upset and—"

"Misinterpret the fact that you tried to kill me?"

"I did *not* try to kill you!"

"So you keep saying."

"Just promise me you won't tell her."

"What's it worth to you?"

"Damn it, Jameison, I—"

"Garrett. Stop calling me Jameison, and I won't say a word to anyone about what happened."

C.J. looked at him suspiciously. "Promise?"

"Hope to die." Solemnly he drew a cross over his heart with his finger. "How about sealing the bargain with a kiss?"

Three

———

"**H**ow about—" C.J. caught herself again, easing her breath between her teeth. "Thank you. Garrett."

He just laughed softly again. He was looking down at her, a little appraisingly, a little…close. C.J. hadn't realized that he'd been moving slowly, almost casually, toward her until he was suddenly just *there,* and she found herself more or less trapped in the angle between the desk and the bookcase.

There was no way she could extricate herself without making it obvious that she was trying to get away from him, and for some reason she didn't want to do that. He was just a bit too self-assured, and it galled her to give him the satisfaction of admitting that he was making her nervous.

Very nervous.

And for no reason at all.

After all, a man who dated the most beautiful women in the entire country—probably the entire *world*—was not going to make a pass at someone like her. Lord knows, she was passably attractive, if you liked flat-chested brunettes with freckles and hair that did as it pleased. But from everything she'd read about Garrett Jameison, he preferred long, tawny blondes with legs up to here and breasts out to there, the kind who showed a lot of teeth when they laughed, which was often, and had thick manes of silky gold hair they kept tossing around.

Women like Chastity O'Roarke, in fact. Who would have found Garrett Jameison very interesting, indeed....

C.J. gave herself a shake, trying to ignore just how much like Chastity's Lord Jamie Kildonan he looked. The same straight, patrician nose, the same thick dark hair, the same mouth, almost hard at one angle, sensual in another. Put Garrett Jameison in satin breeches and a loose-fitting shirt of white silk, tie a sword around his waist and put a good horse under him, and it would be like having Jamie Kildonan come to life and step right off the cover of one of Bertie's books.

She realized, suddenly, that he was looking down at her expectantly, as though he'd said something and was waiting for a reply. "Excuse...me?"

His gaze wandered with comfortable thoroughness, touching her features one by one, moving down the sweep of her bare throat, her shoulders. "I said, you look very different tonight."

"Different?" Her voice was almost a croak, and she was finding it difficult to breath properly.

He was standing too close to her, and the room seemed very small and crowded and hot, and she couldn't catch her breath properly. The warm, heavy air was filled with his cologne, an oddly erotic mélange of leather and smoky oak casks and fine whiskey, with an underlay of something mysterious and exotic that made her think, inanely, of moonlit alleys in Zanzibar or Tangiers. The kind of forbidden, darkly erotic places where you'd find the same kind of man....

"The dress," he was saying. His voice seemed to wrap itself around her, blending with the heady scent of his cologne and the distracting warmth radiating from his body as he leaned, just imperceptibly, toward her. "Your hair. Your perfume..." He smiled. "Different."

"I, um, we—we'd better go in now." The words came all in a rush and she felt a hot blush infuse her cheeks, feeling dizzy and awkward and indescribably silly. "To dinner, I mean. Th-they'll be wondering what's happened to us...."

She made the mistake of looking up at him and found her gaze captured and held by eyes as golden as a cat's. The barest hint of a smile brushed his mouth, not quite mocking and yet not entirely teasing, either, and then, casually, he drew back and away from her, and C.J. managed to drag in a ragged breath, her knees unmistakably weak.

Squaring her shoulders, she drew in another deep breath and looked up at him again, praying the dim light cast by the desk lamp would hide the heat in her cheeks. "I think I should warn you," she began hoarsely, "that... well, that Bertie has designs on you."

"Designs? That sounds intriguingly decadent."

"She... oh, Lord!" C.J. pressed the back of one hand against her cheek. "This is so embarrassing!"

"Why don't you just say it and get it over with." His voice sounded oddly tight.

"It's just that she probably told you things about...well, about me. Heaven knows what, but she... may have given you the wrong idea. About my, um, availability, I mean."

"Are you telling me you're *not* available?"

"That isn't the point. It's just that she has this habit of inviting men out here to... well, to meet me."

To her relief, Garrett just smiled. "I had a feeling there was more to this dinner invitation than met the eye. When she told me she had a grandniece staying here, I sort of figured..." The smile widened, gentle and not at all unpleasant. "I take it she's doing a little matchmaking, is she?"

C.J. nodded unhappily. "She's incorrigible! She's convinced I'm never going to meet a man and fall in love on my own." In spite of herself, C.J. had to smile. "I suspect your reputation as one of the world's foremost bachelors has given her ideas we could both do without. It'll probably be easier if we just play along with her. You don't have to worry that I'll . . . well, take things the wrong way or anything."

He nodded slowly, his gaze holding hers in that disturbing way he had. "So, in other words, I'm safe."

"As houses."

"Too bad."

C.J. blinked. "Excuse me?"

His slow smile could only be called beguiling. "What if I don't want to be safe, C.J.?"

"I—" C.J. blinked again, uncertain of exactly what he meant. And then, suddenly, she realized he was simply flirting with her. It would be second nature for a man like this. She smiled, realizing belatedly that she was blushing again and, for an instant, wishing she were the type of woman who could flirt back. "I, um, think we should get back now. I can look for her walking stick later."

He laughed, his eyes crinkling at the outer corners. "You intrigue me, C.J. Carruthers. I can think of a dozen things I'd rather do with you this evening than go in to dinner, but dinner it is." He gazed down at her, his mouth wearing a smile she found about as reassuring as a shark's. "And I think that's your great-aunt's walking stick by your hand."

C.J. looked down and found herself face-to-face with the grinning gargoyle that made up the handle of Bertie's oak cane, wondering how it had gotten there. "Yes...yes, it is."

"Come on. I'm starved—let's go and eat." He put his hand lightly on her back to guide her around the corner of the desk, and C.J. could have sworn he'd somehow slipped his hand beneath the fabric of her dress to touch bare skin, the jolt it gave her.

"And you don't have to worry about your great-aunt's matchmaking," he murmured as they walked to the door. "Any ideas I have along those lines will be entirely my own."

Which wasn't', C.J. thought with growing panic, what she wanted to hear at all! She tried to move away, but he kept pace with her easily, and the heat and pressure of his hand seemed to increase as they walked toward the dining room, until C.J. was convinced she'd carry the imprint of his fingers for life.

Three days later he hadn't made a damned bit of headway.

Garrett leaned against the wide stone seawall that ran along the foot of the estate grounds and stared at the long, lazy swells sweeping in from the gulf. They'd spill up onto the hot beach with a boom, then slide back in a tumble of foam and swirling sand. It was relaxing, almost hypnotic—and it wasn't doing a thing to ease his irritation.

He'd come out here figuring that C.J. would be the easy part, and Parsons Industrial the challenge. But getting a handle on the Parsons family-run corporation had been fairly straightforward. It was C.J. that was giving him the headache.

Because it was hard to woo a woman, never mind trying to win her, when the most you saw of her was the occasional fleeting glimpse, and that only at a distance.

It was like stalking some rare and exotic bird. He'd walk into a room and catch a subtle hint of her perfume on the air, or hear a soft footfall in the corridor, or hear her musical laugh—except when he turned to look, she'd be gone. A ghost would leave more tangible signs.

Or maybe he just wasn't trying hard enough.

He mulled the thought over, testing it for truth.

Oddly enough, he found himself lying awake at night, faintly troubled by what he was doing. Even with Bertie's encouragement, the whole business left a bad taste in his mouth.

Although why, he had no idea. Bertie loved her grand-niece deeply, a blind man could see that. Her motives were from real concern about C.J.'s future and security, and although her solution was far from ideal, it was a pretty good compromise between romance and hard-nosed practicality.

So why was he feeling so guilty?

It wasn't as though he was taking advantage of C.J. in any real sense of the word. He wasn't even—technically—seducing her. That would mean luring her into bed for his own pleasure and not caring that she'd be hurt, but that wasn't going to happen with C.J. He'd keep his word...he *would* be the best damned husband he knew how, and she'd never know about his deal with Bertie.

And for his part... hell, Bertie was right. It *was* time he was married.

Past time, probably. There was a point in a man's life when he went from acceptable bachelorhood into something a little less respectable, and he was getting close to it. The eternal-playboy image didn't cut it these days, and, in fact, could prove a decided liability in the business arena. Common wisdom had it that if a man didn't have what it took to make a secure and stable marriage, how could you trust him with a million-dollar corporation?

He thought idly of his father, ignoring the little tremor of anger. After his wife—Garrett's mother—had died, he'd turned into a pathetic old fool, ricocheting from woman to woman like a moth in a roomful of candles. Part of it had been grief, Garrett could buy that. But not the rest of it. Not the seemingly endless parade of beautiful young women that had sauntered through his life, each the "right" one until she proved otherwise, all drawn to him by the Jameison name, the Jameison money, the Jameison power. Each liaison had been more widely publicized, the media loving the spectacle of a fifty-two-year-old millionaire making a fool of himself over every gorgeous young thing he set eyes on.

Two or three of which had even managed to dupe him into marrying them.

Garrett realized his fists were clenched and consciously relaxed them, managing a grim smile. Thanks to him, the damage had been minimal to all but his father's pride. And heart. Stringent premarital contracts had protected his father's money and property and business assets, and when these brief forays into wedded bliss had fallen apart, Garrett had always been there to make certain the now ex-wife went on her way without causing trouble.

At times it had seemed like a full-time job. That, and trying to keep the business together as his father started to neglect it more and more in his search for the perfect woman.

Garrett took a deep breath, eyes narrowed on the horizon. Looking back, he didn't know which he'd resented more—the responsibilities he'd been forced to take on at twenty-two, or the embarrassment of having to watch the man he loved publicly humiliate himself with one failed affair after another.

Looking for love, he'd said.

And if that's what "love" was, Garrett thought with a humorless smile, God preserve him from it! All it had done for his father was turn a strong, decisive and capable man into a simpering fool, vulnerable to every gold digger who came his way.

Including this last one, Garrett reminded himself with sudden annoyance, irritated at the fact that he was thinking of her at all. Krystal Pilaski. Or, if you'd been fortunate enough to catch her show in Las Vegas: Krystal Hart, exotic dancer.

He pushed himself away from the seawall, swearing under his breath, and turned to look up the gently sloping lawn to where C.J.'s small bungalow sat tucked into the cooling shade of gumbo-limbo and Australian pines.

Admit it, he taunted himself. You're buying into this crazy deal because—down in those dark corners of your mind a man only half admits to—you're scared of becoming just like him. Scared of waking up one day and discovering you've turned into a lonely old man assuaging that loneliness in a series of empty, meaningless affairs with women who want only the prestige of the name and the pretty things your money can buy.

He shivered slightly. Not quite like his father, he reminded himself wearily. At least, God knows, *he* was smart enough not to confuse it with "love."

Smiling a little at his own whimsy, he turned and set out to find his wife-to-be.

Lord Jamie Kildonan, border bandit, scoundrel, lover, was being extraordinarily difficult for some reason. His scowling, handsome face glowered out of the canvas at her, those brooding dark eyes holding hers with what she could have sworn was disapproval, and C.J. sighed and stepped back from the easel, frowning at the oil painting she'd been laboring over for most of the afternoon.

And laboring was the right word, she thought with some exasperation. Usually her painting was sheer luxury, a few minutes of self-indulgence stolen out of each day when she could set aside the real world and simply immerse herself in the rich brocade of her own imagination.

But not today, obviously. There was simply no way she could get those storm clouds the right color. They looked more bruised than foreboding, and Jamie, leaning indolently against an outcrop of rock, seemed to be looking at her with the studied impatience of an actor waiting for the stagehands to get the scenery right.

"All right, all right," she muttered at him. "I'll try again tomorrow."

Although at this rate she was never going to get it done in time for Bertie's birthday.

Maybe because she didn't want to give it away, she thought as she started wiping the brush on a paint-smeared rag. It was silly, but the more she worked on the painting, on Jamie, the more important it became to her. Caught up in the fantasy she often lost herself for hours, half day-dreaming, half wishing...

What? That the magic—and Jamie—were real?

C.J. smiled slightly and finished wiping the brush clean. Maybe, in a way, she did. Heaven knows, she'd met few real men who could compete—none even half as handsome and dashing and darkly dangerous. Certainly none who were likely to come riding out of the night and sweep her up and carry her off as Jamie had Chastity in *Chastity's Revenge*....

She found herself gazing contemplatively at the painting. It wasn't just the sky she was having trouble with. Jamie...something about Jamie's mouth wasn't right.

Strange, how she'd never noticed until just this moment that she'd gotten his mouth all wrong. It was too thin lipped, too hard. Jamie's mouth was more appealing than that, softer, more...sensual. And his eyes...weren't his eyes a lighter brown, almost amber...?

That's enough! C.J. hauled her wandering mind back to the present and put the brush away, then started cleaning the palette, annoyed with her own undisciplined thoughts. She was spending altogether too much time these days worrying about the color of Jamie Kildonan's eyes, the shape of his mouth, whether she'd gotten his wind-tangled hair just the right shade of chocolate brown.

Or maybe it didn't have a damned thing to do with Jamie Kildonan at all, she advised herself irritably. Maybe it had to do with another man. One a little closer to home; one a little more real.

Garrett Jameison.

Even his name made her heart give a thud. What in heaven's name was she going to do with him?

The knock at the door, coming on the heels of that thought as it did, made her jump. It could be any of a handful of people: Winthrup; Cook, with her regular twice-weekly resignations; one of the maids; Bertie's accountant; even Bertie herself. And yet, even as she was walking across to answer it, C.J. had the distinct feeling that there was only one person who would choose that particular moment to knock on her door....

And so wasn't particularly surprised when she pulled it open and found herself face-to-face with the man himself.

He, on the other hand, *did* look surprised.

"If you're looking for Bertie," she said perfunctorily, starting to close the door again, "she's not here."

"No—I was looking for you." He recovered quickly, she'd say that much for him. He stood gazing down at her as though she was the most pleasant thing he'd seen all day. "I just didn't expect you to answer the door."

"Why wouldn't I? It's my door."

"You've been avoiding me."

It was true, but C.J. saw little point in admitting it. So she just shrugged and turned back into the room, leaving the door open so he could come or go as he pleased. Sooner or later she was going to have to deal with this whole situation, but not right now. She needed to think about it some more. Get used to it....

"Do you mind if I come in?"

"If you want," she hedged, not looking at him. She'd discovered that it was hard to look at him and breathe at the same time, something that made as little sense as everything else these days. Just one more thing she was going to have to figure out.

It wasn't exactly an invitation, Garrett decided as he followed her inside and closed the door behind him. But it was the closest thing to one he'd gotten from her since he'd been on Paradise. Maybe things were looking up.

Shoving his hands into the pockets of his casual cotton slacks, he wandered into the big, sun-filled room, giving a low whistle as he looked around. Where his Green Cottage was all dark wood and English antiques and small leaded windows, C.J.'s bungalow had been opened up into one large room. It was filled with wicker furniture and scatter rugs and dozens of thriving big plants, with enough windows and skylights to make you think you were standing outdoors.

Everything was white and pale yellow, with touches of pink and lime green. On the far side, two shallow steps led up to a raised area that angled across one corner and was, he couldn't help noticing, dominated by a massive brass bed covered with ruffled white linens and a mound of frilled pillows. Over it, hung at graceful angles, were three colorful kites, tails wafting gently in the breeze coming through the French doors leading to the patio. They looked as though they were adrift, held up only by air and magic, as graceful and light as tethered rainbows.

Another facet to the mysterious C.J. Carruthers he wouldn't have guessed. "Nice place."

"I like it."

"More private than living up at the house, I guess."

She turned an unfathomable look his way. "Yes, it is."

He strolled across to an antique Italian writing desk big enough to skate on and looked down at the computer, modem and laser printer. "I thought you worked out of Bertie's office in the house."

"Normally I do. But I figured you and Bertie would want some privacy while you worked out the details of Emmett Royce's job. That *is* what you're doing, isn't it—replacing Emmett?"

"More or less." He glanced around at her. "What has Bertie told you about it?"

"Precious little." There was a hint of irritation in her voice as she started gathering up tubes of oil paint and tossing them into a wooden box. Then she sighed suddenly and offered him a tentative smile. "Bertie doesn't think I can understand the complexities of big business."

"Do you?"

"I understand enough to know that my cousins have turned Parsons Industrial into a force to be reckoned with, and that they're more interested in the bottom line than in any social ethics concerning some of their investments and holdings." The corners of her mouth tipped up again. "Enough to know that Bertie was right in choosing you to take over her interest in it."

"Oh?"

Her smile widened and she shoved her hands into the pockets of her wheat-colored cotton shorts and leaned one hip against the desk. "My uncle and his two sons figure that, with Emmett gone, they're home free. They've never taken Bertie very seriously. She's just this nutty aunt who wanders up to New York now and again to meddle in things she doesn't understand and give them lectures on honor and morality they ignore. They think Bertie will simply replace Emmett from within the company, and that they'll be able to run roughshod over whoever it is. But I doubt," she added with a soft laugh, "that they'll run over you."

There was something about the way she was looking at him, direct and just a little speculative, that made him wonder if she knew more than she was letting on.

Which wasn't likely. There were only two people who knew about the true extent of his deal with Bertie—she wouldn't have told C.J., and he damned well hadn't.

Forcing himself to relax, he strolled across to the fireplace. It was framed in carved marble and he paused to admire it, then turned his attention to the collection of medieval weaponry hanging on the walls above and around it: pikes, a couple of English longbows, swords of various sizes and antiquity, arrows, a variety of crossbows.

He glanced around at her, mouth half-open to comment on the collection, and found her staring at him from across the room, her expression thoughtful, maybe even a little assessing. It made him forget what he'd been about to say and he quirked a questioning eyebrow, thinking idly that she got more beautiful every time he saw her. "What's wrong?"

"Wrong?"

"You were staring."

"Oh." She blinked. "Was I?" Her smile was faintly rueful. "Sorry. I was just thinking about...something."

"Me, I hope." It was glib and obvious and not very inspired, and it occurred to Garrett that his heart wasn't really in it.

C.J. didn't seem to notice. "About Bertie, actually." To his surprise, she wandered across to stand beside him, gazing up at the wall of weaponry. "About how much I owe her for all she's done for me."

She said it quietly, almost to herself, and Garrett found himself watching the play of sunlight in her dark hair, wondering what it would feel like to run his fingers through it.

He'd find out soon enough if things went the way they were supposed to. Although the thought gave him absolutely no pleasure to speak of. All he felt was a kind of sadness, part wistfulness, part resignation. And a hell of a lot of guilt. She was too nice, he thought absently. Too nice to be locked into a loveless marriage for his convenience and Bertie's peace of mind....

He gave himself a shake and smiled at the top of her head. "She's a remarkable woman, all around."

"Yeah." She smiled fleetingly. "Although she's gone downhill this year, I think. She fell last fall and hurt her hip and was in bed for nearly a month, and she never seemed to get all her old zip back."

"It takes me all my time to keep up with her now," Garrett protested. "She goes blasting around the estate in that wheelchair like a Formula One driver."

C.J. laughed, her eyes warm with amusement. "It's a customized job—she got some kid from the Fort Myers stock-car club to come over and soup it up for her. I'm not sure what he did, but she's been a menace in it ever since."

"Speaking of being a menace..." He grinned at her and nodded at the display of armament. "I'm glad all you came after me with the other day was that crossbow."

She winced. "I didn't apologize for that, did I." She looked up at him through her lashes as she said it, eyes soft and as warm as sunlight on sand, her smile a bit flirtatious, a bit shy. "For what it's worth, I am sorry."

It would have been the easiest thing in the world to make a move for her in that moment. Nothing that would frighten her—fingertip against cheek as though brushing away a stray hair, hand on shoulder, the seemingly accidental brush of thigh against thigh. Just the first touch, the first breaking down of barriers, of social taboos. After the first, the second would be natural, even expected. And after that...

Frowning, he deliberately kept his hands in his pockets and broke her gaze, turning to look up at the weapons. "You a collector?" She was making it too damned easy!

"Not intentionally. They're props for publicity tours and some of the cover art mainly, although I've never figured out why her publisher thinks Bertie wants them cluttering the place up." She wandered over to stand beside him. "The crossbow I had the other day was left over from a costume party a local writers' group hosted for her last year."

"You're quite a markswoman."

"I've fooled around with it a bit. I was in here painting that day and it was lying on my desk. When I saw you through the window, I grabbed it without even thinking. It was only after I'd shot at you and you disappeared that I started to realize I might be in serious trouble...but by then it was too late." She gave a wry laugh. "I don't mind telling you I scared the wits out of myself. When you grabbed me, I was just thinking about coming back here and calling the police and telling them I thought I'd murdered someone."

Garrett had to laugh. "You managed to scare me pretty badly while you were at it."

She grinned up at him. "Want to take it home as a keepsake?"

"I don't know about the crossbow, but having one of those broadswords casually lying on the table at a board meeting might come in handy."

"You don't strike me as the kind of man who's easily intimidated."

"Only by beautiful women wielding crossbows."

Four

It made her blush very slightly, and for half a heartbeat Garrett felt ashamed of himself. The breeze coming through the open patio doors ruffled her silken hair slightly and carried her scent to him, a subtle hint of jasmine he found distracting. And, very suddenly, he caught himself wondering if her skin was half as soft as it looked, and what she'd look like naked in moonlight, and how she'd feel in his arms...and told himself, very carefully, that it didn't matter. It wasn't about that. It wasn't about that at all....

Again he turned away from her, gazing up at the framed posters on the adjoining wall. They were bursting with color and action, with rearing horses and armies in full battle dress and castles in flames. And in the foreground of each, the same flame-haired woman dominated the entire cover. She was beautiful, her tangled red hair cascading around her arms and shoulders, breasts half-bared, eyes sultry and dangerous.

Her male companion was the same from poster to poster, darkly handsome and more often than not half-naked himself, with rippling muscles and a burning, sardonic gaze that promised unspeakable things should he ever get his hands on her.

"So who's the lady with the incredible set of. . ." He gestured eloquently. "Cheekbones. Chastity?"

"Yes. These are enlargements of the art proofs for some of Bertie's covers."

"Interesting."

"The . . . cheekbones, or the covers?"

He grinned again. "Both." He saw the oil painting then, sitting on an easel by the window, and strolled across to it.

The man staring back at him through dark, brooding eyes was the same man as in the posters. He was standing with one foot braced on a rock, his woven cape thrown back across the near shoulder, one hand resting on the ornate hilt of the sword hanging from his waist. His hair was long and windblown and he was staring out of the painting as though searching for someone, a faint frown etched across his strong forehead.

"You're doing this." He looked at C.J. curiously and was surprised to see a hint of color wash across her cheeks.

"It's a birthday present for Bertie. It . . ." She shrugged carelessly, not quite meeting his eyes. "She always says the cover artists get it all wrong. So I thought..." She shrugged again, looking uncomfortable.

"You're very good."

"You don't know much about art, do you."

He had to laugh. "Only as an investment. I leave the details to my broker."

"Well, I can guarantee you'll never see a C.J. Carruthers turn up in your portfolio. I'm a dabbler—good enough to enjoy myself, not good enough to be a threat to the art world." She smiled. "Which is all right. I do it to relax, and if I were any good I'd probably have to take it seriously, and there'd go the fun.''

"And what else do you do for fun?'' He asked it carelessly, turning his head to deliberately look down into her eyes and smile at her. It was a well-calculated smile, ingenuous and warm and filled with possibilities. And it made him feel, for just a split second, like a crook.

To his surprise, it didn't have the effect he'd thought it would. He'd expected her to blush and look away, flustered and a bit off balance, giving him the advantage. A little teasing, a little flirting...from everything he knew about her, C.J. Carruthers should be a pushover.

Except there was something cool and a little watchful in the Aegean blue eyes locked with his, and for half a moment he again wondered if she was on to him. But then, like a breeze blown away by morning mist, it was gone.

She lowered her gaze and laughed, shrugging, and when she looked up again, her eyes were teasing. "I swim, I walk on the beach, I putter in the gardens when the gardener's not around to chase me out.'' The smile flashed again, easy and completely captivating. "I...oh, let me see. I collect kites, as you can tell—I take one down to the beach now and again and fly it. I listen to music. I go across to Fort Myers and shop and spend time with friends. I explore the island. I read. Just the normal, everyday kinds of things.''

"Any chance of doing some of these normal, everyday kinds of things with me while I'm here?'' He said it casually, not wanting to push her too far too fast.

"I wouldn't have thought you'd have time.'' She tipped her head back to look up at him, smiling, and he found himself thinking that if it had been anyone else, he'd think she was flirting with him. "Bertie seems to be keeping you pretty busy with all that PI stuff.''

"Not so busy I can't steal an hour or two.''

She shrugged delicately, her smile playful. "How about stealing a whole afternoon?''

Not wanting to look too easy, he pretended to give it serious thought. "I can probably swing it."

"I'm going over to Fort Myers tomorrow to do some banking, and if you're interested, you can tag along. We can have lunch somewhere."

In some perverse way, it annoyed him. He'd almost hoped that she was going to make it harder than this. That she was going to force him to use every bit of his ingenuity and charm to win her. Instead, it was starting to look as though she was going to be the easiest conquest he'd ever made.

Or maybe he just annoyed *himself,* he thought irritably. Maybe this whole damned scheme annoyed him....

He hauled in his wandering thoughts and smiled, forcing himself to remember why he was doing it. Why it was in everyone's best interests, including C.J.'s, that she fall in love with him.

He grinned. "I'd like that. Don't get me wrong—the food's fabulous here—but I *am* getting tired of seafood crepes."

"What, after only three nights?" C.J. gave a snort of laughter. "Don't worry, it's temporary. Cook's just trying to make a point. She and Bertie had an argument, but it'll blow over in a day or two and we'll be eating like kings for weeks to make up for it. Then Bertie will say something that will set Cook off and we'll go through the entire routine again." She grinned happily. "Just part of normal life as we Paradisians know it."

Garrett had to laugh. "And what does a person have to do to become a resident of this strange and wonderful land, anyway?"

She shrugged. "Marry into the family, I guess."

Garrett's heart gave a distinctly guilty thump as her smile widened, her eyes filled with sudden mischief.

"I *am* the only eligible Parsons offspring these days, you know. Crossbow and all."

"A daunting prospect."

"Mmm." She nodded, the smile still flirting around the corners of her mouth.

"A man would have to be pretty determined to take on a challenge like that."

"Or a little crazy," she said with a soft, teasing laugh.

"I've been called both." His grin matched hers.

"So I've heard." Her gaze held his almost challengingly. "But I imagine Bertie knew that before she asked you here."

Garrett went very still. "What do you mean?"

She shrugged carelessly. "I was just talking about your work with PI, Mr. Jameison. What else would I mean?" She met his gaze steadily for a second or two, then, almost abruptly, some of the laughter went out of her eyes. A frown flickered across her face where mischief had played only a moment before, and Garrett had the uneasy feeling he'd just missed something. Something that could have been important.

Still looking introspective, she walked toward the elegant writing desk. "I'm afraid you're going to have to excuse me—I have a ton of work to do this afternoon. I got caught up in my painting and lost track of time." Her smile was rueful as she gestured toward a cardboard carton sitting beside the desk that was filled almost to overflowing with what looked like hundreds of envelopes in every imaginable size and color. "The latest batch of fan mail. Bertie's publisher shipped it up yesterday."

"You and Bertie handle all that yourselves?" Garrett gave a whistle.

"I have an assistant who comes in on Fridays to handle *just* fan mail, but I like to sort through it myself first. There are always a few from regular fans Bertie likes to answer personally, and now and again there's a crank letter—I like to keep track of those so I can spot any repeater and pass it on to the police. There's only been one so far, thank heaven, and it turned out to be harmless, but you never know."

"It must keep you busy."

"This is the easy part. I'm her business manager, her personal secretary, her typist, her publicist and about six dozen other things. Between typing up each day's work, keeping track of her appointments, going over book contracts, fielding phone calls, staying in touch with her agent and her editor, answering correspondence, juggling publicity tours and autograph parties and speaking engagements and interviews..." She gave another one of those delightful laughs that seemed to fill the room with merriment. "It sounds as though I'm complaining, but I love it!"

"I'd say your work with Bertie rivals running PI."

"But a lot more fun."

Garrett grinned. "It's all a matter of perspective."

Her gaze held his with a curious intensity for a moment, then she smiled and nodded. "I've found most things are, Mr. Jameison."

"Garrett," he said dryly. "We have a deal, remember?"

"Yes, I suppose we do." She looked across the wide desk at him, and for a moment Garrett swore he could read a hint of defiance in her eyes. Maybe even subtle challenge. "But deals get renegotiated all the time, Garrett. I have a feeling that this one is no exception." And then she smiled again, almost sweetly, and sat down, reaching for a stack of papers lying to one side of the computer.

The rest of the day went slowly, as far as Garrett was concerned. He spent most of it sequestered in Bertie's main-floor office surrounded by computer printouts and strategy plans and financial reports and personnel records, reading and reviewing and cross-referencing until his eyes crossed.

Finally—and with *great* reluctance—he opened his briefcase and took out the reading glasses that had been sitting there, untried, since he'd picked them up more than three weeks ago.

Reading glasses, for crying out loud!

He rammed them on, angry at his body's latest betrayal, and found himself thinking with some hostility that his hair would probably be the next to go, good genetics or not. Then it would be what...his waistline? Then his knees. Scratch those weekly tennis games, he thought grumpily. And the running. And the occasional workout at the gym.

He was getting old, damn it.

Once, in an unguarded moment, his father had told him that facing his old age alone was the one thing that terrified him. All the joys of his past—being married and much loved, holding his newborn babies, hearing the laughter of his children ringing through the years of his life—nothing could erase the fear of facing those final years with none but his own companionship.

It had irritated Garrett more than it should have. He'd walked out of the room impatiently, remarking that being alone was preferable to being made a fool of by the shoals of barricuda-like women who always seemed more than willing to make an old man's life less lonely.

He'd been ashamed of the comment later, remembering the flash of hurt on his father's face. But for some reason that conversation had haunted him. He contemplated his own future occasionally, seeing himself rattling around in that big Miami condo for the rest of his life. There had been a time when the prospect had given him considerable pleasure. But more and more, it seemed, it left him a little chilled. More so after his younger brother and his wife had had their first child....

"Enough of *this!*" Garrett shoved the chair back angrily and got to his feet, rubbing the back of his neck as he looked at his watch. Practically midnight. Not an unusual hour to find him still working, especially when something as big as PI came his way, but he knew a lost cause when he saw it. All he'd been doing for the past hour or two was day-dreaming and fidgeting, so he might as well just call it a day.

The house was quiet and still. He turned off the light and pulled the office door closed behind him, realizing everyone had gone to bed long ago. As he walked into the kitchen he could hear a radio or television playing very faintly and realized it was coming from the staff quarters in the far wing. So someone was still up. Cook, perhaps, plotting her next evening's revenge on the household.

Smiling, he was just going to unlock the door leading from the kitchen out into the back garden when a movement in the corridor caught his eye. And in the next breath, he saw a man's dark-garbed figure move stealthily toward the wide, curved stairway leading up to Bertie's suite of rooms.

He took one step toward the telephone hanging on the nearby wall, then swore under his breath. The nearest cops were in Fort Myers, and even the fastest police cutter wouldn't make it out here in under twenty minutes.

They didn't have twenty minutes. Swearing again, he stepped across to the big knife block sitting by the stove. It was bristling with Cook's collection of razor-sharp knives and he grabbed one. And, wishing fervently that it were one of Jamie Kildonan's stout Highland swords instead, he headed for the door, thinking a little inanely that if he got himself shot playing hero it was going to play hell with Bertie's plans . . . not to mention a few of his own.

But as he moved silently into the corridor outside the kitchen, he stopped dead. He could see the stairs clearly from here, rising in a gleaming arc of polished hardwood like some surrealistic sculpture. And he could see the intruder, too, halfway up, caught in the moonlight spilling through the fan window above the main doors.

Winthrup.

Garrett leaned forward to get a better look. Pajamas. Winthrup was in pajamas and robe and floppy slippers. And he was, no doubt about it, heading straight for Bertie's suite of rooms.

I may be dying. . . .

A little chill darted down Garrett's spine and he took a step forward, opening his mouth to ask Winthrup if he needed a hand, if Bertie had taken suddenly ill, if—

He was whistling. Winthrup was whistling.

"Well, I'll be damned." Grinning broadly, Garrett stepped back into the shadows, not wanting to be caught inadvertently spying as the elderly man knocked softly on the door to Bertie's suite.

He pushed it open without waiting for a reply and went inside, and Garrett, still grinning, headed back to the kitchen. You sly old devil, he thought admiringly as he replaced Cook's knife and let himself out into the warm, soft darkness of the night. So all wasn't quite what it seemed on Paradise, after all.

He was still laughing as he walked across the wide flagstone patio off the kitchen, then through the arch in the rose trellis that screened the patio from the Olympic-size swimming pool. He'd been out here before at night and had always paused a moment to take in the beauty of the floodlit pool with its surrounding statuary and vine-wrapped pillars. The pool and deck were done in intricately patterned tiles that were almost Moroccan in design, with hints of the Orient and Middle East tossed in for flavor, rich with reds and blues and golds.

But it was the design on the bottom of the pool itself that fascinated him the most, a montage of life-size mermaids frolicking with three dolphins, golden hair spilling across the tiles, eyes glowing a deep cerulean blue, naked bodies slender and lithe. It was an incredible work of art, done with imagination and wondrous skill, and he never tired of it.

"My great-grandfather brought two artisans from Malta to do that mural," a soft voice said behind him. An instant later C.J. appeared at his elbow, as silent as a cat on the cool tiles. She was wearing a one-piece bathing suit the same deep, shimmering blue as her eyes, cut high on each hip and

low in the back, where it was held together by a cobweb-
bing of narrow straps.

It was as sedate as hell in one way, Garrett found himself
thinking distractedly, but the sexiest thing he'd seen in years.
Or maybe it was just the way she filled it out, all sleek fe-
male curves and silken tanned skin and those incredible legs
that just went on forever. Or maybe—

"It caused quite a scandal at the time, having bare-
breasted women sprawled out in plain view like that."

Garrett started guiltily, then realized she was talking about
the mosaic on the pool bottom and *not* the distinctly inap-
propriate images he'd been conjuring up in the privacy of his
own mind. Not daring to meet her eyes, he simply nodded
sagely and hoped she took his reticence as artistic awe.

"A delegation of local ladies even tried to convince him
to have an artist paint little frocks on them." She looked up
at him, grinning mischievously. "Rumor has it great-
granddad's reply sent them scampering for home and the
topic was never mentioned again."

Garrett had to laugh.

"And that chunk of glass in the middle one's belly button is supposed to bring good luck if rubbed just the right
way."

"The whole estate is like something out of a dream, part
old-world England, part Italian baroque, part...hell, I don't
know. Oriental. Indian."

"What you're trying to say is that it's garish and tacky
and a spectacular example of consumerism run amok," she
teased with a laughing, upswept look. "And you're right.
The entire island is proof that money can't buy good taste.
Although—thank heaven—things have improved since the
days when there were live tigers and bears wandering the
gardens, and entire herds of mainland deer and wild boar
were brought over for great-granddad's famous hunting
parties." She gave a shudder.

"It must cost a fortune to keep up."

She smiled. "Ever the businessman. And, yes, it does." Her smile turned wistful and she gazed up at the huge old house. "It gets a little more run-down every year, and I guess sooner or later we're going to have to face reality and either start major renovations or simply move out."

"I can't see Bertie being happy anywhere else."

C.J. shook her head slowly, still looking at the house, her expression a little bleak in the moonlight. "Things don't last forever," she said quietly. "Not even Paradise."

There was something about the way she said it that made him frown slightly, thinking about his father. *You can't make time stand still,* he'd said not long after Garrett's mother had died. *You can't make it the way it was.*

Garrett shook it off, annoyed at how the thoughts intruded when he least wanted them. "Little late for a swim, isn't it?"

"It helps me sleep."

She walked across to the edge of the pool, a blue-and-white towel tossed over one shoulder, and Garrett felt his mouth go dry. Moonlight burnished her shoulder, the long sweep of her bare back, the curve of her thigh.... And to his surprise, as he watched her he felt the first faint tingle of arousal, that peculiar tightening in his lower belly and groin that was more instinctual than deliberate, the male animal's automatic response to some stimuli he wasn't even fully aware of.

With luck, it would last. It would make the whole thing easier on both of them if he didn't have to feign this part of their relationship, too....

She was out of her mind if she thought this was going to work, C.J. told herself numbly. Even if it *were* possible to seduce a man like Garrett Jameison, this wasn't the way to go about it.

Problem was, she didn't *know* how! Everything she knew about the fine art of flirting she'd learned from Chastity O'Roarke, and it hadn't prepared her for something like

this. Chastity, heaven knew, scarcely had to do a thing to
have men falling all over themselves. A couple of long, over-
the-shoulder glances, the slow pass of her tongue over her
lips to moisten them, a half turn to show off those lush
breasts that were always straining at the lacing of her bodice and heaving indiscriminately at every little excuse. . . .

Hell, C.J. thought irately, the woman just had to *breathe*
to be seductive! She spared a glum look down at her own
swimsuited front. *Her* breasts, on the other hand, had never
heaved in her life, indiscriminately or otherwise, and the
only thing they were likely to strain was credibility. So how
did she imagine for even a moment that she was going to be
able to knock Garrett Jameison, inveterate bachelor and
playboy extraordinaire, off his firmly planted feet by
prancing around in the moonlight in this ridiculous swim-
suit? Instead of showing off her charms, it was only high-
lighting the fact she didn't have any.

"You can join me if you like." She said it before she could
chicken out, and accompanied the offer with a sliding glance
over her shoulder she hoped he'd interpret as encouraging.

And as his eyes locked with hers, her heart literally
stopped beating. He'd been watching her the entire while,
she realized in horror—and watching her in a way that made
her feel very suddenly like something small and succulent
dropped in a tiger's cage. His eyes were narrowed slightly,
thoughtful, almost speculative, and the expression on that
lean handsome face equaled anything Chastity might have
seen on Jamie's.

And it scared her half to death.

For a moment, she nearly ended it then and there. She
was *way* out of her depth here, playing with the kind of fire
she'd only read about, toying with things that, once loosed,
might be beyond her control. There were entire worlds of
experiences and emotions and feelings she'd never even
glimpsed before, and suddenly—faced with the reality of
what she was doing—she started to panic.

But only for a moment. Before she did something foolish—like run away and hide—C.J. tore her gaze from his and stepped to the edge of the pool. Not letting herself think about those hot amber eyes locked on her back, she launched herself into the moon-silvered water in a long, shallow dive that carried her nearly a third of the way up the length of the pool.

Five

She surfaced in a flurry of bubbles and gave her head a shake to clear her eyes, not daring to look behind her, then took a couple of leisurely strokes toward the far end. The water was like liquid silk against her skin and she concentrated on that, telling herself that she was doing the right thing.

It was time. Time to think seriously of marriage, of a family. Of the future. Paradise wasn't going to last forever. And only children never grew up.

Kicking gently to keep herself afloat, she smoothed her soaking hair back from her face and looked around at Garrett, intending to say something frivolous and suitably silly—and found herself staring at nothing.

He wasn't there. She stared stupidly at the end of the pool where he'd been standing, then felt the blood rush to her cheeks in embarrassment as she realized he'd simply continued on to his cottage, obviously discounting her invitation for a midnight swim as the idiocy it had been.

Of course he wouldn't have joined her. He'd been fully clothed and there wasn't a pair of swim trunks in sight, for one thing. And besides, why would he waste his time? The Garrett Jameisons of the world did things their way and on their terms, and the last thing this particular one needed was some silly, infatuated woman flinging herself at him just because—

Something fastened around her right ankle and in the next instant she was pulled underwater. She caught a glimpse of strong, tanned male shoulders moving leisurely below her before she was released, and in the next heartbeat she shot to the surface in an explosion of bubbles, sputtering and gasping for breath.

"Sorry." His voice was just a purr of sound close to her ear. There was an accompanying chuckle, throaty and lazy, the touch—a caress almost—of fingertips on her hip, her waist. Then it was gone, and when she turned clumsily in the water to face him, no one was there.

He surfaced a scant three feet from her, grinning, and C.J. gazed at him in sudden consternation. "Wha-what are you doing?"

"Taking you up on your invitation."

"But…but what are you wearing?" The question was out before she could catch herself, and she listened to the words in an agony of renewed embarrassment. "I mean—"

"It's a little late to be worrying about that, isn't it?" His teeth glinted in the moonlight in that lazy grin. "You can come over here and find out, if you really want to know."

"I don't." She was regaining some of her composure, thank heaven, and gave her head a careless toss to get her hair out of her eyes, not having the faintest idea of what to say next.

A light clicked out in one of the windows on the second floor high above them, and C.J. smiled, glad of the distraction. "He's late tonight. I guess he didn't want to go up until you'd finished working and were out of the house."

"Winthrup?" Amusement ran through Garrett's voice and he wiped the water from his eyes with his hand and gazed up at the now-dark window. "So you know."

C.J. laughed, scissoring her legs gently to stay afloat. "Of course I know. She's my great-aunt."

"How long has it been going on?"

"As long as I can remember." He looked at her in surprise and C.J. smiled mischievously. "Twenty years, at least. And no one's supposed to know, by the way, so keep it under your hat."

"Not supposed to know? After twenty years?"

"Winthrup wants to protect her reputation," C.J. said dryly. "All the staff knows, of course, but we pretend nothing is going on. That's one reason I moved out to the bungalow a few years ago, just to make it easier for them. And the rest of the staff never ventures into the main part of the house in the morning until after Winthrup is up and dressed. There have been a couple of close calls over the years, but everyone's used to the charade by now so it's just second nature to avoid embarrassing encounters."

Garrett was still laughing, looking bemused. "Do you think he'll ever make an honest woman out of her?"

"I keep hoping. But Bertie can be amazingly old-fashioned at times—she's afraid of how it will reflect on me if she marries her butler." She lay back in the water, letting herself float on a sea of stars. "As long as they're happy, I don't care."

Garrett didn't say anything, just stared up at the darkened window thoughtfully. And C.J., glad of his distraction, turned and swam away from him as casually as possible. Below her, the three mermaids frolicked and played with their dolphin friends, their smiles wise and mysterious and just a little self-satisfied, as though they knew the answers to questions she'd never even thought of asking.

On a whim, she took a deep breath and dived hard for the bottom. The lights hidden around the pool bottom bathed her in their pearlescent glow, and reflections from above fluttered and rippled along the tiles. She gave a final kick to carry her the last distance and reached out to touch the faceted mock sapphire embedded in the center mermaid's navel.

Nothing happened—no jolt of electricity, no flash of insight, no clap of thunder. And yet she felt strangely reassured, as though this silly ritual, held over from childhood when just reaching the stone was a major accomplishment, was a good omen.

She shouldn't have been surprised when Garrett's hand and sun-browned arm appeared suddenly beside hers, yet her heart gave a definite thump. He caressed the stone with his fingers, then grinned at her, looking a little otherworldly with his thick hair fanning out in the water and the lights and moonlit reflections sculpting the muscled contours of his lean body.

He was, she was relieved to note, wearing his briefs. His stomach was hard and flat, his abdomen trim, his chest strong and wide and densely furred, and he was so healthily, erotically, unsettlingly *male* that C.J. had another moment of raw panic.

But before she could react, he reached out and settled his hands very lightly on her waist, then gave his legs a gentle kick that headed them both for the surface. They rose slowly, trailing bubbles as they let their own buoyancy do the work, and C.J. let her hands rest on his forearms, telling herself there was no reason for her heart to be pounding the way it was.

She was so close to him that she could see the flecks of green in his eyes, the crescent of a scar just under his left eyebrow, another fainter one across his chin. He had a strong, hard-planed face, each feature sharply defined, the angle of his jaw stubborn and uncompromising. Except for his mouth, C.J. thought inanely. He had Jamie Kildonan's mouth, strong and firm and yet with enough sensuous fullness to his lower lip to keep a woman awake nights just thinking about it. Imagining what it would be like to—

They broke the surface and C.J. took a deep gulp of air, giving her legs a kick to keep her head above water and getting them all tangled up in Garrett's. Her thigh slid between his and she felt the muscles in his legs tighten convulsively, tried to pull back and found the impetus of her own kick pushing her against him instead, so they collided in a clash of hips and thighs more intimate than anything Chastity O'Roarke herself could have orchestrated.

C.J. distinctly heard Garrett suck in his breath and realized as she floundered against him that she was only making things worse. Finally she simply went motionless and, as she'd hoped, they drifted gently apart. And, after another moment or two, she remembered to breathe again.

One of Garrett's hands was still resting on the upper flare of her hip, warm and strong and undemanding, and it was only when he'd lifted the other one to cup her chin that she realized what he intended to do. She watched in mute astonishment as his face neared and in the next instant his lips were on hers, lightly at first, just a teasing touch that made her head swim, then more firmly, pressing hers apart gently. She felt the silken thrust of his tongue against her teeth, just a momentary hint of intrusion that was more erotic for its promise than the actual taste of him, then he lifted his head and that was the end of it.

She could have cried out for the sudden loss, wanting more, wanting . . . just wanting.

But he kicked away from her gently instead, letting his hand fall away from her hip, his fingertips caressing her through the fabric of her swimming suit. There was electricity in that fleeting touch, and magic. She could feel it coursing through her veins like sweet poison, and she shivered suddenly, every cell in her body vibrating as though he'd just run a bow over the strings of a harp.

"It's late." He said it quietly, almost as though it was an apology, and C.J. wondered what he was seeing in her eyes.

Probably no more than she was seeing in his, she thought dazedly. Something had happened . . . was happening . . . between them. Something she didn't understand, wasn't sure she wanted to understand. "Yes."

"Dinner tomorrow night. . . ."

"Yes . . ."

He reached toward her and she lifted her hand to his and for one magical heartbeat their fingers braided, his touch like fire. Then, almost regretfully, he drew his hand free and turned and swam leisurely toward the near end of the pool, pulling himself out of the water in one graceful, lithe move. Water cascaded off his glistening body as he bent down to gather up his discarded clothes, then he walked across and disappeared into the deep shadows under the rose arbor. And, a long while later, C.J. realized she was still holding her breath and eased it out in a long, unsteady sigh.

"He took you to dinner last night" were the first words out of Bertie's mouth as C.J. walked into her great-aunt's office two mornings later. "Jerome tells me you and Garrett held hands on the launch coming back to Paradise and I saw the two of you kissing in front of Periwinkle House a little after midnight—quite a lengthy process it was, too. You seemed to be enjoying it. Does this mean what I think it means?"

"It means you're the most shameless snoop I've ever met," C.J. said when she could finally get a word in. She dropped a stack of letters on Bertie's big desk. "If you can spare a minute or two from minding *my* business to taking care of some of your own, these letters need your signature."

"Touchy, aren't we," Bertie offered drolly, squinting a little against an acrid stream of smoke lifting from her slender imported cigarette. "Have you slept with him yet?"

"I'm not even going to dignify that with an answer." C.J. plucked the cigarette from Bertie's fingers and stubbed it into the cut-glass ashtray.

"I guess that means no." Bertie gave a snort. "You're not getting any younger, my girl. By the time I was your age I'd sown enough wild oats to—"

"I do not want to hear about your wild oats," C.J. said with calm precision. "The galleys for *Chastity Unbound* came in this morning—they need any changes by Friday."

"Where did Garrett take you for dinner?"

"Just a seafood place on the waterfront. And he didn't take me to dinner, we just ate together. It didn't mean anything."

"And I suppose you're going to tell me that kiss in front of your door didn't mean anything, either." Bertie gave another snort. "I've seen lifeguards revive drowned swimmers in less time than you two were going at it."

"Keep it up," C.J. told her pleasantly, moving the stack of letters squarely in front of Bertie and slapping a pen down on top of them. "It's just more ammunition to have you carted off to the Hillcrest one of these days."

"You wouldn't do that," Bertie replied quite serenely as she picked up the pen. "You love me altogether too much."

"Try me," C.J. said sweetly. "Start signing."

A small smile flirted around Bertie's mouth but she refrained from saying anything else, to C.J.'s relief, and simply started signing her name to the letters with a flourish, pausing now and again to read one that particularly caught her eye or add a few words under her signature.

C.J. shoved her hands into the pockets of her white cotton shorts and strolled across to the big window overlooking the front gardens. The gardener was trimming back an overly exuberant azalea and C.J. watched him absently, her mind wandering.

It had been like this all morning. She kept finding herself sitting at her desk or standing at a window without the slightest idea of how she'd gotten there or what she was supposed to be doing. She'd made two phone calls and, somewhere between the time she'd dialed and when the person at the other end had answered, had forgotten why. She'd found herself standing in the kitchen not long ago, pen in hand, and hadn't the faintest idea of where she'd been heading, or even why.

What she had no trouble at all remembering, though, was the previous evening in Fort Myers with Garrett. He'd met her a little after four and they'd wandered around a couple of art galleries and boutiques, not really shopping as much as simply talking. Dinner had been at a dockside restaurant where they'd sat outside overlooking the marina, talking and laughing until Garrett had suddenly decided he wanted to take her dancing. And, ignoring her protests that she wasn't dressed for it, that she couldn't dance, that she'd embarrass them both, he did just that.

Then there had been a drink at that dark, intimate little bar he'd heard about, where, for the first time that evening, he'd meshed his fingers with hers and had tugged her close to him. And, later, had kissed her, his mouth warm and familiar and tasting of brandy. He'd kissed her again as they'd stood on the wharf waiting for Jerome to bring the launch in to take them back to Paradise, and again under the awning on the foredeck.

She'd been half-drunk with the taste of him by then, intoxicated by the nearness and warmth of him, the touch of him. And when they'd finally gotten to Paradise and had said good-night to Jerome and had strolled hand in hand up the path to Periwinkle House, C.J. had made up her mind to ask him in. To toss caution to the four winds and just let whatever happened happen, feeling wild and reckless and wondrously uninhibited.

There had been an instant when she'd thought he would. They'd stood there in the moon-silvered shadows by her door for a long, taut moment, eyes locked, and C.J. could see he was tempted. It could have been innocent enough, a drink, a few minutes more of conversation and easy laughter, and then he could have simply gotten up and left. And yet, in some deep part of her, C.J. had doubted it would be that easy. And knew, too, that he was as aware of that as she was.

So, in the end, she wasn't even particularly surprised when he just shook his head, his eyes caressing her face like the touch of a lover's hand.

"I don't think that would be a good idea, C.J.," he'd said softly. "Not a good idea at all...." And then he was kissing her again.

His mouth tasted of brandy and sea salt and it settled over hers with satisfying thoroughness. It wasn't a teasing kiss this time, or even a tender one, but as certain and forthright and uncompromising as the man himself, and she responded to it eagerly, any shyness she might have felt with him long gone.

And he touched her then, the weight of his hand just a slow caress along the long sweep of her back, the curve of her hip, molding her gently to him so they stood fitted as closely as one, and she could feel the unmistakable stir of his body as his tongue swirled and moved against hers in dangerous, hypnotic rhythms, could hear his breathing catch very slightly as she let herself melt against him.

His hand moved slowly up the flare of her rib cage until his thumb rested against the outer swell of her breast and she sighed, wanting him to touch her more intimately, her body suddenly aching with the *need* to be touched. But he didn't. Instead, he drew his hands from her slowly and stepped away, his eyes glittering a little in the moonlight.

And there was something in the way he was looking down at her that made her shiver with sudden, delicious anticipation, knowing as certainly as she was standing there that he wanted her—that in his mind he was already making love to her, his lean, muscled body joined to hers, moving strongly on her, within her, making her cry out again and again, his hungry gaze holding hers with the same intensity as it was now as he—

"Good night, C.J." His voice was rough and he drew in a deep breath, then expelled it through clenched teeth.

C.J. swallowed, feeling dazed and disoriented. "Good night," she whispered, her voice sounding strange, as though it were coming from far away. As they stood there for another moment, eyes locked, she wondered if she was supposed to be saying something, then realized that she'd already said everything she needed to say, and all without uttering a single word.

A smile touched his mouth, and then he turned and walked away.

"—going to stand there daydreaming all day, or mail these letters?" Bertie's voice brought C.J. back to the here and now with a jolt, her heart still racing with the memories. She could taste Garrett in her mouth, could feel the gentle caress of his hand on her back, her shoulder, the curve of her hip....

She shook it off and turned away from the window, hoping her face wouldn't betray what—who—she'd been thinking about.

She walked across to retrieve the letters, sparing a half moment to reach over and slip the unlit cigarette out of Bertie's fingers. "I'm going to find who's smuggling these things in to you, you know, and when I do, he's toast."

"I'm seventy-six years old," Bertie snapped. "If smoking was going to kill me, it would have done it by now."

"Dr. Willerson says—"

"Pig's ears! I've outlived two doctors already, and I'll outlive Willerson, too. Winthrup, where are you? *Winthrup!*"

"You'll probably outlive all of us," C.J. said calmly, "but as long as I'm still around, you will *not* smoke, got that?"

"You used to be quite a nice child," Bertie advised her balefully. "What happened?"

"Twenty-odd years of trying to keep you out of trouble."

"He's quite a catch, you know."

"Dr. Willerson?"

"Don't be thick! You know very well I mean Garrett."

"I'm ignoring that."

"Rich, with plenty of smarts and a solid future ahead of him. Marvelously handsome. Well built, too—have you noticed those shoulders? Yes, of course you have. And a good deal else, I should imagine, while the two of you were splashing around in the pool the other night." She gave a salacious chuckle.

"I'm ignoring that, too. Have you told my cousins about your decision to bring Garrett into the business yet?"

"Yesterday." There was an evil chuckle. "Bertram was on the phone the minute my fax hit his desk, screaming blue murder. And those three greedy sons of his were threatening to fly down to talk some sense into the old lady—that's me—before I did something foolish."

C.J. grinned. "And I imagine you handled the situation with your usual aplomb and graciousness."

"I told 'em to go to hell," she said with satisfaction. "Garrett's been on the phone with them all morning, getting a few things straightened out. *Winthrup!*"

C.J. nodded, looking at Bertie seriously. "They'll try to have you declared incompetent, you know. You ought to call Willerson and have him prepare a statement verifying that you're of sound mind and body and all the rest of it."

"So now I'm of sound mind and body, am I? Five minutes ago I was as mad as a hatter, according to you."

C.J. smiled patiently. "You're looking tired. Have you been sleeping properly? And are you taking those vitamins that—"

"Yes, yes, yes!" Bertie made shooing motions with her hands. "You're fussing, C.J. I don't like it when you fuss. *Winthrup!* Where *is* that man! He deliberately ignores me, you know. He's probably standing around the corner smirking while I—"

"You called, Madam?" Winthrup appeared from nowhere, his expression serene.

"Called? *Called?* I've been shouting myself hoarse for the past ten minutes! I want a drink."

"Hemlock, Madam?"

"You're fired, Winthrup!"

"Yes, Madam. Tea, you said?"

"A *large* whiskey."

"A very small whiskey," C.J. put in firmly. "And no seconds. Make sure you lock the liquor cabinet behind you, Winthrup—she sneaks in and helps herself when she thinks no one is watching. And someone is buying cigarettes for her again. Put the word out that when I find who's responsible, I'm going to personally take him out into the gulf and toss him overboard."

"Yes, Miss," Winthrup said with a small smile. "And if I may be so bold, I'd be only too glad to help."

"Torture, that's what it is," Bertie muttered, glowering at them. "One of these days I'm going to do myself in just to spite the lot of you. A good bonfire should do the trick. I'll stack all my books around me and go up like Joan of Arc!"

"Match?" asked C.J. sweetly.

Six

Bertie's reply was short and pungent, and C.J. was still laughing as she walked out the door.

And right into Garrett Jameison's arms.

"Mmm. Nice." His teeth flashed in a teasing grin as he slipped his arms around her with enthusiasm. "This is the best thing that's happened to me since I got out of bed. In fact, I'd say you've just improved my day by about two hundred percent. Good morning."

"Good...grief!" This as she watched the letters she'd been carrying go sailing off in a variety of directions. "I mean," she amended a little dizzily, breathing in the heady scent of cologne and shampoo and warm male skin, "good morning."

"In spades." He gave a throaty chuckle, seeming in no hurry to let her go. "I was just thinking about you."

"You were?" It was hard to breathe, all tangled up in his arms like this, with those smoky brown eyes locked with hers and that oh-so-familiar mouth near enough to touch.

"Mmm." His smile widened. "I find myself thinking about you a lot, as a matter of fact."

"You do?" A little breathlessly.

"Uh-huh." And with no warning at all, he bent down and kissed her, just a fleeting pressure of his lips on hers that lasted no more than a heartbeat and yet, C.J. was sure, sent tremors through the very ground they were standing on.

What else would account for the fact that her knees nearly gave way? He released her a half instant later, that reckless smile still sending its own variety of tingles through her, and she stood there unsteadily, trying to catch her breath. "I, um," she said very calmly. "I . . . that's interesting."

"I thought so." His grin turned slightly wicked. "Dreamed about you last night, too."

"Oh . . ." Faintly.

"How about taking this afternoon off and going for a walk? Or riding—we could take a couple of the horses out to the Indian mound and look for arrowheads."

"A walk?" She was starting to sound demented, C.J. thought desperately. What in heaven's name was *wrong* with her! "I mean, I can't," she said much more firmly. "I've got a zillion things to do this afternoon and—"

"All the more reason to take a couple of hours off."

"I . . . can't." She didn't even have to feign the regret in her voice. "Garrett, I can't—really. Bertie's agent just faxed down a draft of a fifty-page contract with enough fine print to tie a team of Philadelphia lawyers in knots, and the publisher needs our answer by Friday."

He reached out and took her hand in his, frowning slightly as he toyed with her fingers. "I enjoyed yesterday evening," he said quietly. "And I guess I'm taking a hell of a lot for granted, but I got the feeling you did, too. I'd like to spend more time with you while I'm here. . . ."

"Me, too," C.J. said softly. She tried to keep herself from fantasizing that it meant more than it did. That his interest in her went beyond just another Jameison conquest.

It didn't, of course. She already knew that. Had already made up her mind to make it easy for him. And yet she felt her heart give a leap when he smiled down at her again and his fingers tightened momentarily around hers.

"Good." He bent down and brushed his lips across hers again, and then, before she could even get her breath back, he'd turned and was striding through the door into Bertie's office.

It was getting harder every damned day to keep his mind on business, Garrett mused hours later. He looked at the mounds of paper cluttering the desk with something that felt almost like distaste. And it scared him a little.

He'd always used work the way some men used golf or fishing, and the tougher the challenge the better he liked it. He was at his best when things were at a crisis point, when the deal could go either way and millions hung in the balance. It was then that negotiations got interesting. Once you got past all the paperwork and the politics, once the lightweights were off the field and it was just the serious gunslingers left and the stakes were as high as they were going to get...that was as real as it got. No compromise. No room for mistakes. And he loved it.

Not that taking over Emmett Royce's position at Parsons Industrial was going to be that kind of a challenge—this wasn't a hostile takeover or even a buyout. He was simply stepping in to handle Bertie's controlling interest in the corporation. Her brother's family would fight like badgers, of course, and there would be a skirmish or two while various board members and other associates scrambled to decide their new allegiances.

But the dust would settle soon enough. He'd oversee a restructuring of the power base, implement a change or two at a corporate level and, once the fun was over, he'd bring in one of his people to run things on a day-to-day basis and go on to something new.

Except ... something was wrong this time around. There was none of the visceral thrill he usually felt, none of the anticipation for the battle ahead. Just a kind of shadowy dread he couldn't even really pin down.

And he knew damned well why. C.J. Carruthers.

Admit it, Jameison, he taunted himself, she scares you spitless. She's not like all the others; there's not a damned thing she wants or needs from you, not the money, not the power, not even the challenge of trying to get you into bed. She's not *after* anything. And that makes her an unknown quantity.

He sighed and leaned back in the swivel chair, tapping his pen on the desk as he stared out the tall narrow windows overlooking the side gardens. It was getting late. The sun was halfway to the horizon already, setting the edges of the melon-and-apricot-colored clouds afire as it slipped into the sea. The row of palms edging the lawn stood like sentinels against the hot sky, looking for all the world as though they'd been painted there, and the azure blue sea behind them sparkled and glittered as the sun caught the long, lazy waves rolling toward shore.

Paradise.

A tap at the door made him glance at it and he smiled with real pleasure when C.J. popped her head around the corner. "Hi. Busy?"

"Nope." He tossed the pen aside recklessly and swiveled the chair to get a better look at her. Liking, as always, what he saw. "Come on in. What's up?"

"Not much." Smiling, she pushed the door open with her foot and came in, carrying a tray laden with a silver carafe, cups and a plate piled high with pastries. "Bertie said you've been doing battle with the other half of the Parsons clan most of the day, and I thought you might need refueling." She set the tray on the desk and the scent of freshly brewed coffee filled the room.

He reached across and took a pistachio pastry as C.J. filled two cups with steaming coffee, adding a splash of cream and a single spoonful of sugar to his, just the way he liked it. He grinned as he took it from her. "Are you trying to make yourself indispensable, or just make me think twice about ever leaving?"

"Maybe both." She grinned and pulled one of the straight-backed chairs nearer to the desk, then sat down with a sigh. "Hope you don't mind if I hide out in here for a few minutes. Cook's resigned again—that's the third time this week, a new record. The gardener caught the dogs digging in the rose bed, and Winthrup found out that the kid who helps Jerome with the launch has been smuggling in booze and cigarettes for Bertie." She combed her thick glossy hair back with both hands, laughing. "This place is like a zoo! Aren't you glad you're here for just a couple of weeks?"

"Oh, I don't know. It has an advantage or two." Garrett held her gaze for a moment, then bit into the pastry. Thinking, idly, that a man could get used to this. And her....

"So I hear you've been talking with my cousins. I suppose they've been threatening to have Bertie declared incompetent, to take the whole thing to court, to do this and that."

"Nothing I didn't anticipate."

"They're all good people, really. They just have to learn that they're not running the show alone." C.J. took a sip of her coffee, looking at him over the rim of the elegant porcelain cup. "It's none of my business, but if it were me, I'd give Gordon and Nesbitt more to do. Just to make it easier to swallow. To let them know you trust them. And when I brought in new blood, I'd do it at a lower level—leave the existing directors in place to reassure everyone. No one at PI is a bad risk, they're just a little...independent."

Garrett nodded again, thoughtfully this time. "You've got a good grasp of the politics involved. Are you as sharp on the actual details of the corporation and its business dealings?''

"I pay attention to what's going on, if that's what you mean. I don't know if I could reel off the name of every subsidiary of every company we own, but I have a pretty good idea of where the money is—and where it's going." She smiled around the rim of her coffee cup. "So if you're planning to pull a fast one, Mr. Jameison, think again.''

It made him laugh, long and lazily, and he found himself just looking at her, liking the way the sunlight slanting through the tall windows haloed her silken hair and highlighted the curve of her cheek.

He thought of the way she'd felt in his arms last night, warm and soft and feeling the way a woman should, of the taste of her mouth, cinnamon and brandy and fire. Of wanting her...not wanting just the arranged marriage and all the rest of it, but wanting *her*. It had caught him unexpectedly, sharp and poignant, and he'd ached to take her to bed and simply lose himself in the sweet innocence of her, the purity of everything she was and everything she wasn't.

It would be easy to fall under her spell, he thought absently. Easy to find himself actually thinking that—

The phone rang just then, blaring through the comfortable silence that had woven around them. C.J. started to get to her feet, but Garrett waved her back down as he grabbed the receiver.

"Jameison," he barked into it. "What is it?"

C.J. took another sip of coffee and relaxed back into the chair, thinking she should probably go down to the kitchen and see how the latest crisis was shaping up.

"You *what?*" Garrett erupted to his feet violently, sending the heavy swivel chair careering away. "What the hell do you mean, *married?*"

He paused, listening, and as the voice on the other end went on, his eyes narrowed dangerously. "Are you out of your mind?" he half shouted. "You can't marry that—no,

damn it, *you* listen to *me!* I knew she was setting you up the minute I set eyes on her, but I never thought you'd actually be gullible enough to fall for it. Don't do a thing—and for God's sake don't sign anything until I get there! I'll fly in tomorrow and have her packed and on her way before—''
There was another pause, longer and even more deadly than the last, and Garrett's eyes started to glitter. "I know you're on your honeymoon," he said with deceptive softness. "But I am not going to let that cheap little—''

The receiver on the other end was put down so firmly that even C.J. heard it and she winced slightly, winced again when Garrett slammed his own down. "He married her."

"Who," C.J. asked calmly, "married whom?"

"My father," Garrett got out between clenched teeth, "just married a Vegas stripper named Krystal Hart."

There wasn't, C.J. decided, a lot one could say to that. Congratulations obviously weren't in order, but sympathy didn't seem appropriate, either. She settled for something midway between and simply murmured a bemused, "Oh."

"God Almighty, you'd think he'd learn! This is the third, no, the *fourth* time he's let some little gold digger get her claws into him. I spent a fortune on private detectives, digging up enough dirt on her that you'd think he wouldn't give her the time of day, and instead . . . !" He raked his fingers through his hair, leaving it in disarray, and started stalking back and forth through the lengthening shadows. "And you can bet he didn't have her sign a prenup, either. That means getting rid of her is going to cost us a damned fortune."

"Maybe she loves him," C.J. offered very quietly.

"She loves the balance in his bank accounts, his stock portfolio, his yacht, his jet, his Platinum Card. You can bet she just loves him to pieces."

C.J. frowned, thinking he was probably overreacting but just as certain he wouldn't appreciate being told so. "So you've met her."

"I've met her," he grated. "Right after he came back from a weekend junket in Las Vegas, and suddenly everything was Krystal this and Krystal that. I flew into Vegas and had a talk with her, although I obviously could have saved myself the trip."

"What did she say? When you went down to see her, I mean?"

"That Dad was an adult and didn't need my permission to live his own life. That she hoped I'd understand, but since I couldn't, to butt out. That I was acting like a jerk because of my unresolved feelings about my mother's death and... oh, hell, she took a strip off me a mile wide."

To C.J.'s surprise he suddenly gave a snort of laughter. "She was probably half-right. I never did forgive him for starting to date so soon after my mother died. It was a betrayal, you know? But, hell, I was nineteen—what did I know? I had college and friends and all the girls I wanted. It never occurred to me that he might just be lonely. That all he was trying to do was find a little companionship."

"And you think that's what he's doing now?"

"That's exactly what he's doing now," he said coldly. "Oh, he thinks he's in love with her. Just like he thought he was in love with all the others. And the one thing you can be certain of is that where there's a lonely, vulnerable man, there'll be a lineup of women all too happy to make him feel better."

"That's the most cynical thing I've ever heard," C.J. protested. "Men and women fall in love all the time. And there's nothing calculated about it—it just happens."

"Love?" He looked around at her as though she'd just beamed down from another planet. "That's the biggest trap of all. A man's at his most vulnerable then—hell, he's liable to do almost anything when he thinks he's in love. And any woman worth her salt knows that and milks it for all its worth."

"I think," C.J. said a little stiffly as she got to her feet and set the coffee cup down, "that I'd better check to see what we're going to have for supper tonight. With Cook gone, it's every man for himself."

He didn't say anything, but something shifted deep in his eyes and for a moment she thought she saw regret on his face, a peculiar wistfulness. But he turned away and walked across to the window as though forgetting she was even there, and after another moment or two she left.

A woman, she told herself very firmly as she headed for the kitchen, would be well-advised to keep her heart under lock and key with Mr. Garrett Jameison. Because if she did actually fall in love with him, it would be the loneliest feeling in the world.

She was still thinking about this a couple of hours later, in spite of her best efforts not to. After she'd left Garrett that afternoon, she'd scrounged up a meal for Bertie and had spent a few minutes chatting with her, then had come out to her bungalow with every intention of getting some work done.

Instead, she'd stood staring at her half-finished painting of Jamie Kildonan, thinking idly that the resemblance between Chastity's pirate and Garrett was more striking every time she looked at him. She'd finally gotten the mouth right, but now she saw that Jamie's eyes were still all wrong…they weren't intense enough, weren't quite the right shade of tawny gold…like Garrett's, she mused, a soft smoky amber one moment and heated brass the next.

She finally shook off her restlessness and settled down with a copy of Bertie's most recent publishing contract in front of her, wishing her mind would quit wandering. Every time she *almost* had the implications of a new clause figured out, she'd suddenly find herself thinking about something else—Garrett, usually, or Bertie—and would have to start all over again.

She finally just gave up altogether. Indulging in a long, hot shower, she pulled on her terry robe and curled up in an easy chair with a fat mystery novel, and had just gotten into it when someone knocked at the door.

"It's open!" She called, not even bothering to look around. "I knew you wouldn't be able to resist my invitation. Two out of three, and then we go to bed, all right? And no funny stuff this time, either."

"Wouldn't dream of it," a seductive male voice purred against her ear. "And two out of three before bed sounds great."

C.J. catapulted out of the chair as though she'd been shot and wheeled around, one hand clutching the throat of her robe, the other brandishing the book like a weapon. "My God, you scared me half to death!"

Garrett just grinned lazily at her, looking very relaxed in cutoff jeans and a gray sweatshirt with a University of Florida crest on it. "Sorry," he said, not looking even remotely sorry. "Does this mean the invitation's off?"

"I thought you were Bertie! We play cribbage now and again, although she cheats like a bandit, and she said she might be up for a game tonight. Unless there was a hockey game on—she's nuts about hockey."

"Pittsburgh at Boston," Garrett told her. "She and Winthrup are watching it in the den, eating popcorn and swearing at the referees. She's got a pretty colorful vocabulary for a seventy-six-year-old lady, doesn't she?"

"I've seen her make teamsters blush. What's that?" C.J. nodded toward the flat carton he was holding aloft. "Smells like pizza."

"Is pizza. Giovanni's Ultra-Deluxe Super Special with the works, light on the anchovies, to be exact. You like anchovies?"

"I love anchovies, but how did you—?" C.J.'s eyes widened. "You didn't!"

"He guarantees he'll deliver anywhere."

"But…" C.J. gave a sputter of astonished laughter. "It's a thirty-minute boat trip out here from the mainland. You're not telling me he delivered a pizza all the way from Fort Myers—it must have cost a fortune!"

"A couple of hundred," he admitted with a laugh. "But it's a small price to pay to have you talking to me again."

"I wasn't aware I'd stopped."

"Not technically, maybe, but things felt a little frosty when you walked out this afternoon."

"Oh." She smiled.

"So are you going to help me eat this thing or not?"

"Absolutely. But I think I'd better get dressed first."

Garrett's slow smile said volumes. "Not on my account."

And C.J., laughing, met his gaze boldly. "Very much on your account, Mr. Jameison." She nodded toward the small open kitchen tucked into the far corner. "You'll find plates in the cupboard, and I think there's a bottle of wine or two in the fridge. There should be something to go with a two-hundred-dollar pizza." Still laughing, she walked across and picked up her jeans and a sweatshirt from the chair where she'd tossed them earlier, and headed for the bathroom.

On one hand, Garrett thought as he uncorked a bottle of French burgundy, it was a shame to drink a one-hundred-and-fifty-dollar bottle of wine with take-out pizza. But on the other, he was having more fun than he'd had in years, and that warranted something.

"What are you laughing about?" C.J. appeared at his elbow suddenly, reaching past him to a mushroom from the pizza and popping it into her mouth. "Ooh—hot!"

"I stopped by the house and tossed it in the microwave for a couple of minutes. And I'm laughing because I can't remember the last time I ate take-out pizza—with or without a great French wine—and just kicked back and had…fun."

"Sounds as though you work too hard. I'll carry the plates and glasses, you bring the pizza and wine."

Smiling, Garrett followed her to the small round glass table set in the bay window overlooking the beach. "You're probably right. But it's been a hell of a long time since I met a woman who'd even *eat* take-out pizza, so there's that to consider."

C.J. just shrugged, concentrating on maneuvering a slice of hot pizza to her mouth without burning herself on the strings of cheese trailing from it. "Sounds as though you need to meet a different class of women" was all she offered, taking a cautious bite from the crust. "Mmm, this was a fabulous idea, Jameison."

"You could be right about that, too," he muttered, looking at her for a thoughtful moment. Hair tousled, no makeup, wearing a simple pale blue sweatshirt over jeans, she was the most beautiful thing he'd seen in years. Being married to her wasn't going to be much of a hardship at all, he found himself thinking suddenly. In fact, being married to her could turn out to be one of the nicest things that had happened to him in a long, long while.

They ate the pizza companionably, chatting about this and that, relaxed and comfortable with each other in a way that bemused Garrett slightly. He wasn't making any effort, that was the strange thing. Whatever was happening between them was happening all on its own, unexpectedly and naturally. Almost, he found himself thinking, as if it was the real thing.

After they'd cleaned up the dishes and had finished the wine, C.J. made coffee and they sat in the quiet of her living room and talked some more, their conversation loose and easy and wandering all over the place, punctuated by laughter and a lively amount of good-natured banter. It was Garrett who finally got up and put some music on, a slow, bluesy number that ached to be danced to, and Garrett who ignored C.J.'s protests and pulled her to her feet and into his arms.

She was a little stiff at first, as though not sure she liked the idea, but as they continued to dance and the smoky, sensual music wove its magic around them, she relaxed against him. And the next step was so natural that he didn't even have to think about it, finding her sweet mouth under his with no effort at all, coaxing it open, kissing her lazily.

They danced like that for a long, long while, C.J.'s arms around his neck, his draped around her slender body, holding her close, lips brushing, teasing, and now and again a deep, slow kiss that would last until both of them were breathless. Then she'd rest her cheek on his shoulder and they'd dance some more, and after a while Garrett found himself wanting to simply pick her up and take her across to the big brass bed and slip her out of her jeans and shirt and make love to her the same way, the slow, deep, lazy kind of lovemaking that lasted all night and well into the next morning.

And oddly, in the end, it was his own desire that stopped him from doing just that. It wouldn't be right, somehow, making love to her when it was all just a charade. He'd have to sooner or later, he knew that, and when the time came he'd make it easy for her. And as good for her as he was able. But until then ... hell, until then it was just cheap seduction, plain and simple. And that was *not* part of his deal with Bertie.

"I've gotta go," he murmured against her ear finally, easing her away from him. "Before this gets completely out of hand."

C.J. stepped away from him, looking flushed and dazed, and she nodded, wetting her lips and drawing in a deep, unsteady breath. "I, um, okay." She looked and sounded as though she'd been wakened from deep sleep, her eyes heavy, voice slightly slurred.

Not even giving himself time to think about what he was passing up, Garrett walked across to the door, his arm draped comfortably around C.J.'s shoulders. "It's been nice." He looked down at her and suddenly they were both laughing, and he tugged her into his arms again, his face buried in her sweet-scented hair. "More than nice. A whole lot more than nice, in fact."

"You could, um, stay for a while...."

"No." He drew back again, even more regretfully this time, and smoothed a strand of flyaway hair from her cheek, her skin like satin under his fingers. Her eyes were wide and shadowed, and they locked with his and he felt something pull wire-taut inside him. "If I stay," he said very softly, "I'm not going to leave until morning, and we both know it. And it's too soon for that, C.J."

"And if I said it was all right?" she said just as softly. "If I said I wanted to?"

He just smiled and shook his head, running his finger along her lower lip. "No. You're not ready yet. You think you are, but its the wine and the dancing and the moonlight talking, C.J. Not your heart."

"But—"

"If we spend the night together, you'll open your eyes in the morning and see me lying beside you, and you'll hate yourself—and me. The only thing you'll be able to think about is getting me the hell out without having to look me in the eye, and you'll spend the rest of my stay here trying to avoid me. So let's not rush things, okay?"

C.J. opened her mouth to tell him that he was wrong, but in the next heartbeat he was kissing her again. His mouth settled warmly over hers and he kissed her with a deep, drugging intensity that was nothing at all like the other times. This kiss wasn't teasing and fun and playful, but the erotic, hungry kiss of a man with more on his mind than simply saying good-night, his tongue tangling sensuously with hers, slippery and hot and coaxing.

A wave of pure, melting desire swept through her and she sighed into his mouth and slipped her arms around his neck again. He pressed her against the doorframe, his hands molding her to him, touching her, caressing her through cotton and denim.

She felt him then, aroused and hard and quintessentially male, wanting her, needing her, and she whimpered very softly and moved against him without even planning to, every cell of her body crying out for that intimate touch. He murmured something and kissed her again, urgently and swiftly, then wrenched back from her with an abrupt, breathless laugh.

Her thigh was still between his and he was still leaning slightly against her, making no effort to hide his body's obvious physical response, simply smiling down into her eyes as though they were sharing a secret.

And it was that—his natural acceptance of his own sexuality, his desire, his physical self—that she loved the most about him, she decided. It was a simple and natural outcome of their closeness that he seemed to revel in as he did in her, and any remaining hesitancy she might have felt vanished then and there.

He stepped back, wincing a little, and they both laughed again, Garrett's eyes twinkling with mischief as he bent down to brush his lips across hers. "Most women would take that as a promise," he murmured. "I hope you're no exception."

It made her frown slightly and she nodded, reality starting, finally, to seep through. And as though he could read her mind, Garrett tipped her chin up so he could look into her eyes, his face serious.

"It's not what you think, C.J.," he said quietly. "I know what you've heard about me and all the women in my life. I'm not going to lie and tell you I'm celibate, but I can tell you I don't take even ninety-nine percent of what's offered, either. For one thing, it's suicide these days. And for another, it's just never been my style. When I make love to a woman, C.J., it has to mean something. Sex is easy. Caring takes some time."

"I, um..." She could feel herself blushing furiously and hoped the moonlight would hide it as she studiously avoided looking at him. "I, um, guess this is probably a good time to tell you that, um, I ... well ... haven't ... you know. Before." He was so silent for so long that finally she couldn't stand it any longer and stole an upward glance through her lashes at him.

He was staring down at her with such a peculiar expression that C.J. hugged herself, certain that she'd somehow ruined it all with that one rash—and completely unnecessary—confession. Surely she could have *faked* it, she told herself furiously. It was hardly brain surgery, after all. A few judicious gasps, a moan or two ... how hard could it be, anyway? No man with his experience would want to bother with a silly, virginal little—

"Never?"

He sounded more bemused than horrified and she dared another upward glance. "Never. It's not...well, that I didn't *want* to. Or even that I haven't had the opportunity. It's just..." She shrugged helplessly. How to explain something she barely understood herself?

"You didn't have to tell me," he murmured, lowering his mouth and nuzzling the downy spot just under her ear. It made her toes curl and she shivered. "But I'm glad you did. I'll make it special for you, C.J. The first time should always be special."

And then he was walking away, starlight glittering in his thick hair, the sea behind him booming up onto the hard-packed sand, and C.J. felt something rush up through her, so strange and frightening and wonderful that she had to swallow.

Be careful, she told herself as she watched him vanish through the arch in the arbor leading to the cottage next door. Be very careful, C.J., or you're going to find yourself in love with that man without even knowing how it happened. And that just wasn't part of the deal.

Seven

He couldn't sleep.

Swearing under his breath, Garrett rolled out from under the covers and swung his legs over the side of the bed, then sat there, elbows on knees, and stared at the entwined flowers woven into the carpet under his feet.

This wasn't the way it was supposed to happen.

Wearily he rubbed his eyes with the heels of his hands, wishing he'd never listened to Bertie's bizarre proposition. Wishing he'd never left Miami. Wishing…oh, hell, he didn't even know what he wished. Or wanted.

He'd thought he wanted C.J. Until tonight. Until he could have had her with no effort at all. If he'd gone with his instincts, he'd be in there right now making love to her, not sitting here in the dark feeling angry and confused and ready to call the whole thing off.

It was the lying that was the worst part. The women he knew were shrewd, direct, fully aware of what they wanted and how to get it. They knew all the moves to all the games,

just as he did. And, like him, they'd play them with no il-
lusions, not being used as much as using—wanting his
name, his power, his money, his influence. Wanting everything but *him*. Which was exactly the way he liked it.

Except, with C.J. it was different. The rules of the game
had changed, and he wasn't even certain how. Or what
happened next.

He should have made love to her tonight, he told himself
coldly. She'd wanted him to, even expected him to. If he'd
learned anything about her during the past week, it was that
she knew her own mind and, for the most part, damned well
did as she pleased.

And he'd wanted to, there was no denying that. God
knew, he still ached with the wanting, the scent of her skin
still clinging to his fingertips like fine perfume, the taste of
her still in his mouth. It took no effort at all to visualize her
lying naked in that wide, wide bed, dark hair atumble
against the pillow, that lithe, slender body burnished by
moonlight and desire. He'd make love to her slowly, braced
on his hands so he could look down into her eyes, and she'd
bite her lower lip and moan softly when he—

Swearing, he reared to his feet, his body responding so
urgently to his own fantasizing that it made him groan with
frustration. He couldn't remember the last time he'd so un-
remittingly *wanted* a woman—physically wanted her so
badly that just thinking about her made him dizzy.

And it wasn't just the sex. There was the rest of it, too—
enjoying her companionship, laughing with her, talking,
weaving the silly jokes out of everyday things the way you
do when you're with someone you like. They were already
talking in that comfortable shorthand that good friends—or
lovers—use. Were already laughing at things that had happened days ago and could be recalled with no more than a
glance, a single word. Were sharing *memories*, for crying
out loud!

And it was scaring the hell out of him. Marrying her was one thing. He'd given his word on that; he'd go through with it. But he was damned if he'd let himself fall in love with her.

And with that, jaw set, resolve steeled, he turned and headed back to bed.

They were all down for breakfast the next morning. Even Cook was there, bustling between kitchen and sideboard with trays and serving dishes.

They had guests, Dr. Willerson and another tall, horse-faced man with that indefinable look of a lawyer about him. Bertie looked very much the lady of the house, happily holding state at the head of the big table with her entourage of small, noisy dogs. She was dressed regally in purple and gold, her hair wrapped up in a turban thing that made her look like the queen of Persia, and she was holding forth on the latest bank scandal while Winthrup hovered discreetly in the background.

C.J. was seated on the far side of the table and she looked up when he came in. Her eyes locked with his for a split second before sliding away, and Garrett was amused to see a blush drift across her cheeks.

Wandering over to scan the breakfast layout, he picked up a warmed plate and started helping himself to scrambled eggs and sausage and fruit. He walked around to sit beside C.J., thanking Cook as she set a brimming cup of coffee in front of him. "Good morning, Miss Carruthers. How are you today?"

"Just fine. And you?"

"Never better. Pass the cream?" She did so, and as he took it from her he deliberately covered her fingers with his, smiling a little wickedly as he caught her gaze. "You look great this morning. Pink suits you."

"I'm not wearing—oh." The pink of her cheeks deepened and she looked away, trying not to smile. "This is going to be awkward. I can tell." She said it softly, although Bertie and her two guests were too involved in their argument to hear.

"All we did was kiss a little."

"I'm glad we—I mean, I want to thank you for not . . . letting it go any further. I think you were right. About how I'd feel this morning, I mean."

"Glad, or relieved?"

She dared, finally, to meet his eyes. "What's the difference?"

"Relieved just means the timing wasn't right. Glad means it never will be."

"Oh." She appeared to give it considerable thought, frowning as she spread marmalade on a piece of toast. "I guess," she finally said, very softly, "that 'relieved' is the right word."

"Thank God for that—you had me worried for a minute. Any chance you can get away later this morning?"

She gave him a look of such outright consternation that he had to laugh. "For a walk, C.J., just for a walk. Relax, will you? I'm not going to pounce on you when you're not looking. We'll go as slow as you want, I promise."

It should have made her feel better, C.J. thought a little desperately. But it didn't. Seeing him this morning, being this close to him, hearing that rumbly way he had of laughing . . . she thought of being in his arms last night, of how easy it would have been to have just let go and let it happen.

She should have *made* it happen, she told herself irritably. Gotten it over with once and for all, before she lost her nerve.

"This afternoon would be better," she murmured.

"I'll try to get loose around two."

"What are you two whispering about down there?" Bertie's black eyes snapped and glittered. "Jameison, are you trying to seduce my grandniece under my very nose?"

"Every chance I get," Garrett said with a lazy laugh.

"Good. She needs some color in her cheeks, a little spring in her—"

"Bertie!" C.J. was on her feet in an instant. "I'll take you into your office where you and Dr. Willerson and Mr. Richardson can plot your plots to your hearts' content. Just what are you up to this morning, anyway? Rewriting your will again?"

"None of your business," Bertie snapped. "And stop being such a prude! My heaven, to think you've got Parsons blood in those veins—it boggles the imagination."

"Your imagination has never boggled," C.J. told her dryly. "And your prurient little mind is one family trait I'm just as glad I *didn't* inherit."

"Pig's ears! You'll come around one day, my girl. All we Parsons women were slow to blossom, but once we did, we redefined the word passionate." She put a cigarette into a long silver holder and gave Garrett an arch look. "I worked in a brothel once. Did I ever tell you that?"

"You did no such thing," C.J. said promptly, whipping the holder away. "If you insist on telling such outrageous lies, Bertie, at least keep them clean, will you?"

"You are beginning to annoy me, child" came the baleful reply. Her hand flashed out and deftly snatched the cigarette back from C.J.'s fingers. It vanished into a pocket. "Go away. I want to finish talking with my doctor and my lawyer—without interruption. Then I want to get back to work. I plan to have chapter ten finished by tea." She looked over the top of her glasses, eyes glinting. "This is where Jamie rescues Chastity from the evil clutches of the samurai warriors sent to bring her to Lord Quang, only to be bushwhacked by—"

"Bushwhacked?" C.J. asked drolly. "Mixing genres now, are we?"

"*Shanghaied,* then. My God, you try me at times! Set upon, is that better?"

"Much," murmured C.J.

"*Set upon* by Turkish pirates. Whereupon Chastity is introduced to the delights of a Turkish—"

"Turkish delights?" This, with a snort, from C.J.

"*Out!*" Bertie roared, glasses slipping dangerously. She banged her walking stick so fiercely it startled one of the dogs and it ran yelping from the room, immediately sending up a chorus of howls from the rest. "My God, I haven't seen such a collection of Philistines since Alaric sacked Rome!"

"Alaric was a Vandal, Bertie, not a Philistine," C.J. said soothingly. "Please at least *try* to keep your history straight. And I'm sorry for upsetting you. Do you want me to take you into your office, or can you manage on your own?"

"Lawrence will take me into my office," Bertie said crisply, not entirely mollified. "And it's a good thing I'm *not* rewriting my will, or I'd be sorely tempted to cut you out of it entirely."

"Yes, Bertie," C.J. murmured, hiding her smile by dropping a kiss on her great-aunt's lilac-scented cheek. "If you get tired, just call me and I'll take you upstairs."

"*Will* you stop fussing over me! I may be old, but I'm *not* daft, so put a cork in it!" But she gave C.J.'s hand a pat as she said it to show all was forgiven. "Now go away, child. I have an entire houseful of people who do little else all day long but watch over me, including Winthrup, who's taken to hovering lately like a maiden aunt. Go, *go!*"

And C.J., wishing she could convince herself that everything was really as fine as Bertie wanted her to believe, went.

She spent the rest of the morning trying to keep herself too busy to think, to worry, but it was useless. And finally she simply shoved Bertie's book contract into a desk drawer and went for a walk along the beach.

It was one of those perfect Florida days when the air currents are just right and the heat haze and ever-present pollution is swept away, leaving the air crystalline, the sky hard and bright, the water sparkling and clear. The breeze was warm but brisk enough to make the palms along the shoreline rustle and clatter, and there was a narrow band of dark cloud running along the horizon where a storm was gathering.

There weren't supposed to be storms in Paradise, C.J. thought irritably. Paradise was supposed to be . . . well, paradise! A place of magic and happiness and serenity, where things never changed and people never got sick. Never . . . died.

She swallowed and took a deep breath, fighting the ache in her throat. Damn it, Bertie, how long did you think you could keep it a secret? Why didn't you just *tell* me! How long do you think you can keep on protecting me?

Struggling not to cry, she shoved her hands in her pockets and started walking again, half-blinded by tears. It would work out, she told herself over and over. It will work out. . . .

Garrett found her, finally, about four miles from the house where the wide, hot beach ended at the edge of the mangrove swamp that made up the entire south and west sides of the island.

The beach was narrow here, just a ribbon of sand separating the water from a seemingly solid wall of lush jungled greenery filled with the hum of frogs and insects and the rustle of leaves. It ended at a narrow inlet of water, across which Garrett could see the tangle of mangrove, roots arching and looping, the water there still and dark and uninviting. As the breeze stirred the tangled trees, bars of shadow and sunlight flickered and shifted in a kaleidoscope of dizzying patterns, mysterious and a little forbidding.

C.J. was sitting in the sun-speckled shade of a sprawling gumbo-limbo tree that hung out over the sand, arms around her updrawn knees, staring out across the gulf. The wind ruffled her cap of dark glossy hair but she didn't seem to notice, and Garrett stood there for a moment or two, just looking at her. Wondering, with more impatience than curiosity, why just seeing her made his stomach tighten in what felt very suspiciously like anticipation.

Which didn't make a damned bit of sense.

He walked across to her finally, and as his shadow fell across her, she looked up slowly. And it was then that he saw the tears.

He knelt beside her, his heart giving a thud of alarm. "C.J.?"

"Oh...hi." She looked away abruptly, giving her cheeks a careless wipe with her arm. "I'm, uh, were you looking for me?"

"We had a date."

"A what?" Her voice was rough, as though she'd been crying.

"A date," he repeated. "To go for a walk. This afternoon."

"Oh. Yeah." She gave him a lopsided, wan smile, then turned her face away and wiped her eyes with her hand. "Sand in my eyes," she whispered. "I...forgot. About our walk, I mean. Sorry."

"What's wrong?" He asked it gently, surprised at how deeply it mattered. "You're crying...."

"No." She swallowed abruptly, the sound almost a sob.

Garrett didn't even know he was going to put his arms around her until he did, but once he'd pulled her gently toward him, he knew it was the right thing to do. She was stiff and unyielding for a moment, keeping her face turned away, and then she gave another little sob and turned into his arms, tucking her head under his chin and drawing in a deep, unsteady breath.

"I'm scared to death," she said after a while, her voice muffled against his shirt. "It's Bertie. Her heart..."

Garrett tightened his arms around her. "Bad?"

"I think so. I finally got that wretched Willerson to admit he'd been treating her for nearly a year. And that it's getting worse. He's . . . worried."

Swallowing a weary oath, Garrett leaned against the smooth trunk of the gumbo-limbo and drew her into his lap, resting his chin on the top of her head. "I'm surprised he told you."

"He didn't want to," C.J. said with a gulp of laughter. "But I convinced him that if he thought Bertie was hard to get along with, he hadn't seen *anything* until he got on my wrong side."

Garrett had to laugh. "I'm beginning to think you have a hell of a lot more of Bertie in you than most people realize."

She was silent for a long while. "I hope so," she finally said, very softly. "I have a feeling I'm going to need it."

Frowning, Garrett didn't bother replying, massaging her shoulder gently with his hand. He'd spent half the day on the phone with her great-uncle and his sons and *their* sons, and it hadn't taken long for him to realize that they thought Bertie was more an irritation than a serious business-woman, and that C.J. simply didn't count at all.

They'd all been bemused when he'd reminded them that C.J. would inherit that contentious fifty-one percent of the company when Bertie died. And when he'd further suggested that she should sit in on the next board meeting, there had been a glacial silence, then one of the sons had laughed and said that he doubted "the girl" would be interested.

Garrett found himself smiling a little malevolently. The entire board of Parsons Industrial was going to get a surprise or two over the next few months.

"That's why she brought you into PI, isn't it?"

He paused very slightly. "It . . . may have had something to do with the decision."

"And me?"

"You?" Garrett repeated casually.

She sat up slowly and pushed a handful of tousled hair off her forehead, smiling a little. "I just wondered where I fit in, that's all."

Careful, Garrett told himself. *Be very careful.* He smiled at her, reaching out to wipe a smudge of damp sand from her face. "I was kind of wondering that myself," he murmured, drawing his fingertip down her cheek. "Because I have to admit that PI isn't the only Parsons family treasure I'm finding interesting...."

Her smile widened. "You're very good at this, aren't you."

"Good at what?"

"At this." She turned her face and kissed his hand, letting her lips linger warmly on his cupped palm. "Making me feel... special."

"You are special," he said quite truthfully. "Very special."

Something shadowed her eyes for a moment, something sad and a little weary. Then she gave a soft laugh and kissed his palm again, looking at him from under her lashes. "As I said... you're very good." And then, with no warning at all, she leaned forward and kissed him gently, her lips wind cooled and tasting of salt.

He caught her by the shoulders and tried to pull her closer, lips parting under hers, welcoming her, but she pulled back and shook her head. "Not yet, Garrett," she whispered. "Soon, but I... I just need some more time. Time to... to get used to the idea... all right?"

She started to stand up, but Garrett caught her shoulders again and turned her to look at him. "You *are* special to me, C.J.," he said quietly, holding her gaze with his, suddenly finding it urgent that she believe him. "I know I've got a hell of a reputation to live down, but you're not just some kind of conquest to me. I don't want you to think..." He gave his head a shake, looking for the right words. "Hell, I don't know. That you're just another notch in Garrett Jameison's belt or something. I meant it last night when I said that's never been my style. And I meant it this morning when I said you've got as much time as you want.''

To his surprise—and consternation—her eyes suddenly welled with tears. ''Thank you,'' she whispered, touching his cheek with her fingertips. ''I never dreamed you'd be so . . . so *nice*.'' The last word was just a gulp and then she was gone, pulling out of his hands, face averted.

He started to get to his feet, but she held her hand out to stop him. ''No,'' she said in a half sob. ''Please, I want to go back by myself. I need time to think. To figure out what I'm going to do. . . .''

Garrett swore wearily and rubbed his face with his hands, wondering for about the five hundredth time why he'd let Bertie talk him into this. Or, more to the point, how he'd let *himself* talk himself into it. It had sounded relatively straightforward at the beginning. But C.J. had been just a name back then, part of a business deal, not even a real person.

But now . . . hell, now she was real and alive and important in ways he was only starting to understand. And vulnerable, he thought dully as he pushed himself to his feet and headed back up the beach. So damned vulnerable. . . .

C.J. dreamed about Garrett that night. Strange, erotic dreams unlike any she'd had before, and they left her aching with a want she only half understood, knowing only that she was breaking her own resolve not to start caring for him. Knowing, too, as she slipped out of bed the next morning with that feeling of wonder-filled anticipation at seeing him again that the whole thing had gone somehow awry.

She hadn't expected this—not the caring, the gentleness, the *tenderness*. Nothing she'd heard or read about Garrett had even hinted at this side of him. And although she was delighted at the unexpectedness of it, it scared her. Because instead of being able to maintain a businesslike approach to the whole thing, it meant she was halfway in love with him before she'd even started. Which wasn't the way she'd planned to handle it at all.

In the end, knowing the kind of man he was made it easier than she'd thought it would be. Although she *had* more or less taken for granted that it would be Garrett who'd be the hunter and she the prey, not the other way around.

Hardly your typical sacrificial virgin, she taunted herself later that same evening. She stepped back from the full-length mirror in her spacious bathroom to take in the results of the past hour, frowning. Not bad. No Chastity O'Roarke, but then, nature had given Chastity O'Roarke more to work with.

A lot more. Frown deepening, C.J. tugged the neckline of the pale blue silk negligee a bit lower. Smooth gleaming shoulders, a swell of upper breast, a hint of cleavage—that was as good as it was going to get.

The negligee was beautiful, a skimming of shimmery silk here, an extravagance of chiffon there, as fine as sea spray. There were insets of handcrafted lace at bodice and hem and sly cutouts and tiny seed pearls. It moved like mist around her as she walked, the chiffon foaming around her calves and ankles so it looked as though she were walking out of the sea, and even to C.J.'s unpracticed eye it looked as seductive as sin.

A caress of perfume across her shoulders, between her breasts, one last sweep of the brush through her glistening hair, a deep breath . . . and she was ready.

He wasn't going to go through with it.

Said aloud, it made him feel better.

The hot, pounding spray of the shower thundered across Garrett's shoulders and he closed his eyes and eased out a taut breath, then started rubbing the soap across his chest and arms.

He and Bertie would have to come to some agreement about his involvement in Parsons Industrial, that was all. But C.J. was out of it. He would not—could not—go through with it.

He'd spent the better part of the past week trying to convince himself otherwise. Trying to tell himself that she would be happy with him, that he'd be a good husband to her, that it was the smartest thing all around to convince her to marry him.

But Bertie was right: he *was* an honorable man. And honorable men did not trick innocent women into marrying them for all the wrong reasons. She'd find someone else, someone who would love her the way she deserved to be loved, and he'd... hell, he'd survive. He always did.

Maybe he'd pick out one of those cool, tailored, aerobically toned, machine-tanned women who strode into his office now and again, briefcase in hand, mind clicking like a calculator, and marry *her*. They'd work up the contract well beforehand, detailing expectations, specifying what each wanted, laying down defaults and penalty clauses. They'd both get what they wanted without any of the risk—she, everything the Jameison name could provide; he, the relief of not having to play the role of perennial bachelor anymore. And neither one of them would be foolish enough to pretend it was love.

He dawdled under the shower longer than he normally did, then rubbed himself down with one of the big blue towels and tied it loosely around his waist before pulling the bathroom door more fully open and stepping into the spacious bedroom in a wreathing of steam. He'd turned all the lights off but the one on the low table beside the bed and the big room was mostly in shadow, scented with the sea.

It took him a moment to realize he wasn't alone. At first he thought the movement near the window was just the curtain stirring in the breeze. And then, with a growing sense of disbelief, he watched silently as she stepped wraithlike into the light.

She was every man's secret dream standing there in something sleek and almost sheer, the light limning the curve of hip and thigh, the swell of a breast, the glossy cap of hair curving around her face.

"Holy...Moses," he breathed in awe. "What are you—?" Stupid question, he told himself dazedly. It was patently obvious what she was doing here. "Oh, C.J. Bad idea, sweetheart. This is a real bad idea...."

To his surprise, she simply smiled. It was a seductive little smile, unlike any he'd seen on that delectable mouth before, and he watched, unable to move, as she walked slowly toward him. The blood was starting to pound in his temples and he knew if he didn't stop this—now, *now*—he was going to do something he'd live to regret.

She was close, so close the warm scent of her wafted around him, that incredible woman scent of oils and expensive lotions and sweet, warm flesh. He swore he could feel her body heat radiating against him like the heat from flame, knew if he ran his fingers along her shoulder it would be like touching silk...knew if he did, it would be all over.

And yet, even as he gazed down into those wide, expressive eyes, he already knew it was over. That all that agonizing in the shower not ten minutes ago had been for nothing, all the good intentions to leave in the morning...empty promises to himself.

This was the only reality—this silken-skinned, sweet-scented woman with eyes the color of bruised violets who was smiling up at him with a smile as ancient as the world itself. Reaching for him now, her touch as light as a butterfly's wing against his chest, her lips moist and slightly parted, lifting for his....

Even as he was fighting it, he knew he was lost. There had never been any question of it right from the start. She needed him and he, in his own way, needed her, and the only question had been when....

"Now" was all she whispered as she stepped into his arms. "Make love to me now...."

She was satin and sin, silk and temptation, and she filled his arms with the sweet perfection of always and forever. Her mouth was honeyed with desire, and as he gathered her up in his arms and took her to his wide, waiting bed, he heard her sigh a little, and smiled.

She'd known. With that ancient wisdom of all women, she'd known things he'd only dimly perceived, his male mind too preoccupied with the stalking games, the pursuit, the promise of plunder. While he'd been pawing dirt and bellowing at the stars, telling the world of his conquest, she'd simply waited quietly, knowing he was hers. Knowing... hell, knowing things he'd never figure out if he lived to be a thousand.

He shucked her out of the negligee gently and slowly, unwrapping her as he would a precious thing, and spent a long and erotic while gorging his senses on the tastes and sensations of her, exploring every silken inch of the body he'd until now only thought he'd known. She was shy one moment and adventurous the next, daring to touch him, to tease him, slowly, slowly unfolding as a flower will to rain, each step giving a little more of herself, growing bolder as his caresses turned smoldering want to aching need.

He readied her long and well, and when he finally eased his weight over her and into the hammocking warmth of her thighs she sighed with pleasure and satisfaction, sighed again as he lowered himself that final, irrevocable distance that has no measuring.

There was that delicious instant of snubbing pressure, the sudden slipping through, that breath-held instant when her eyes widened with the realization of what was happening and she went motionless, as though listening to some inner wonderment. Then she gave a slow smile and a contented purr of encouragement and, permission granted, he let himself sink farther down into the encompassing warmth of her.

He drew it out as long as he could for her, not knowing if this, their first time, would even bring her the pleasure he wanted for her. And so when it finally came for her, he smiled a little fatuously, feeling inordinately pleased with himself as he felt the first tiny tremors run through her, knowing even before she did when it started to end.

Her breath caught suddenly and he felt her stiffen slightly as though with utter astonishment, and then it swept through her on an uprushing wave so fierce it made her arch under him with a low, startled cry, fingers clutching his shoulders as though she was afraid of being swept away. He held it as long as he could, letting it ebb and then bringing it back for her until each individual pulse beat of sensation blended into one long drawn-out, shuddering release that left her limp and sobbing for breath.

He started moving again and she muttered something that was half plea, half dazed denial and he managed a hoarse, abrupt laugh and simply let himself go, his own completion so satisfyingly sudden that he lifted onto his forearms with a low growl of pleasure, his body shuddering under its onslaught.

And then there was the long tumble down the other side, both too exhausted and spent to even talk, bodies all in a humid tangle, the sheets long since gone, pillows scattered to the four winds. She snuggled against him, head tucked under his chin, one arm up under his shoulder, the other around his waist, one of his thighs locked between hers, and he could feel tiny little aftershocks run through her now and again.

And as he lay there with her cradled in his arms, he found himself thinking sleepily that maybe it wouldn't be so bad after all, letting this woman into his life. He'd taken greater risks. And often it was the riskiest deals that had given him the most.

He turned slightly and rested his cheek on hers, the tangled curls along her hairline wet and salty. "Marry me," he murmured against the moist curl of her ear.

"Mmm?" She shifted against him sleepily, sighing like a sun-warmed cat as she nuzzled his throat. "Whatzat?"

"Not whatzat," he teased, setting his teeth across her earlobe. "I just offered to make an honest woman out of you, and—you're not paying any attention to me, are you?"

"Hmm." Her tongue made an interesting foray along the side of his jaw. "Am, too...."

"Marry me, C.J. Carruthers. Be my wife, my bride, my better half. Have my children. Wash my socks...."

"Wash your own socks" came the amused reply from under his ear. "And I thought you'd never ask."

"Is that Carruthers talk for yes?"

"Hmm."

"C.J....?"

"Hmm?"

"You're playing with fire, sweetheart. I wouldn't do...that...unless you're prepared to carry through."

"Hmm."

"C.J.... C.J., I don't think—oh, the hell with it." He rolled her onto her back with a mock growl and pinned her wrists together. "Are you going to marry me?"

"Will I have to keep doing this sort of thing if I say yes?"

"Absolutely," he told her sternly. "Two or three times a day, maybe."

"In that case, I don't see how I can possibly refuse."

Later—much, much later—C.J. found herself replaying that part of it again and again. He'd made it so...easy. So plausible. She'd heard him ask what needed to be asked, heard herself reply. It had been like watching a play, the action scripted and rehearsed, the words uttered by someone else.

In the end, after it was over, she felt astonishingly calm. His lovemaking had been more wonderful than anything she could ever have imagined, and lying tucked into the angular curves of his body, listening to the slow, strong beat of his heart, it was easy to pretend.

It would be all right. She did love him, there was that, anyway. It would make up for a lot. And who knows, maybe in time he'd even learn to love her... even just a little. And he'd never have to know.

He turned to her during the night and they made love in the surreal glow of moonlight, and this time it was, unbelievably, even better. He touched her and caressed her and pleasured her as though she was the most precious thing he'd ever known, and it was sometime during that long, love-filled night that the last of her doubts drifted away.

"I love you," she whispered, gazing up into his pale golden eyes and knowing, with a kind of splintering, aching happiness, that it was the truest thing she'd ever said.

And Garrett, smiling, simply lowered his mouth to hers and kissed her gently.

It was still real in the morning.

When Garrett awoke to an empty bed, he had the sudden, unpleasant feeling that the whole thing had just been a dream—an extremely *vivid* dream, but still a dream. Then he heard the sound of the shower and rolled onto his back in a tangle of woman-scented sheets and grinned with the unexpected pleasure of it.

He was no saint. He'd been here before, had gone through the morning-after rituals. But it had never felt like this before.

And he had the sudden, lightning-bolt realization that it was going to be like this every morning of his life. Waking love weary and gritty eyed from lack of sleep, the taste of her still in his mouth, his body still tingling from the remembered touch of her skin.

They'd made love the last time not an hour ago, the early dawn just caressing the sky, and he'd drawn her across him that time, had lain heavy eyed and languorous as she'd knelt astride him with newfound boldness. Her body had seemed suddenly more ripe, her breasts heavier and fuller, dark tips swollen, the flare of her hips more lush. The tousle-haired tomboy was gone, and in her place was a sensuous, sexually aware creature whose body wove magic on his and whose dark eyes were filled with the erotic wisdom of a thousand generations of womanhood.

She'd watched him the whole time, eyes heavy lidded and smoky, a small mysterious smile on her lips as she'd moved and undulated and writhed over him, teasing him, coaxing him. Her own experimentation had nearly gotten away with her near the end when she'd all but forgotten him, lost in her own suddenly inflamed needs, seeking her own release with the same urgency as she sought to give it. And he'd let her find her own pace, her own rhythms, certain there could be no more erotic thing in the world than watching your woman please herself as she's pleasing you.

She'd arched back finally with a soft, fierce groan and he'd clasped the backs of her thighs tightly, holding her to him as the shudders ran through her again and again, and then she'd finally sagged forward and down into his arms, half sobbing, her body humming like a bowstring.

Just thinking about it made his body respond with a vitality that mildly astonished him, and as he felt the familiar tightening in his lower belly, he rolled out of bed and padded toward the bathroom. She was humming bits of some opera he half recognized, and when he drew the glass doors to the shower open, she glanced around, momentarily disconcerted.

Then, blushing, she smiled. "Good morning."

"Incredibly good," he purred as he stepped into the big shower stall with her and closed the door behind him. "I figured I should do my part to help conserve Florida's dwindling water supply...." He took the bar of soap from her hands and lathered it slowly across his chest, down his arms.

Hot water cascaded down her slender, tanned body and he looked at her with frank approval, loving the way her waist nipped in, the sleek curve of hip and thigh, her small, firm breasts with their lush dark tips, the slight swell of her belly, the shadowed triangle at the juncture of her thighs... loving every tidy inch of her.

Still grinning, he reached out a large soapy hand and started lathering her shoulders and she smiled and moved a little closer, looking up at him through her lashes as she let her fingertips trail across his chest. "Conservation of our water resources, is that all this is about? You, uh, didn't have anything else in mind, did you?"

Her breasts were full and heavy in his hands and he soaped them slowly, feeling her nipples tighten as he teased them, seeing her eyes grow smoky. "I imagine we can come up with another idea or two...."

"I think," she murmured, her hand moving with exquisite precision, "that we already have."

Garrett had to fight for breath as she caressed him with all the shy delight of any new lover and he moved against her encompassing hand gently. "I didn't bring anything in with me, C.J.," he murmured. "So we either go back to the bedroom to finish whatever we start in here, or..." He smiled. "I get creative...."

"I love creative," she whispered, giving him one of those smoky, upswept looks that made his stomach knot. "But we don't have to worry about it now, do we? Unless you've changed your mind about wanting to marry me."

"I haven't changed my mind." He swallowed, wondering how she managed to make him feel so tongue-tied with no more than a look, a smile, a touch. "But kids are a big step, C.J. It might not happen right away, but..."

"So love me and let's not worry about it," she murmured, lifting onto her toes and kissing him. "I want you making love to me. I want to feel you touching me...touch me, Garrett. Touch me...."

Not saying anything, he knelt slowly in front of her, running his soapy hands over her belly, taking his time as he lathered her, then down her thighs, around her taut little bottom. She sighed and leaned against the wall, arching her back as he ran his hands up her ribs to cup her breasts, then drawing his flattened palms down the fronts of her thighs and up again, touching her gently with his thumbs and feeling her start with a tiny indrawn moan.

He eased his hands between her thighs and nudged them apart and she murmured something thickly and grabbed his shoulders for balance. As he nuzzled her lower belly she gasped his name and her fingers tangled in his soaking-wet hair.

But she didn't pull him away and a moment or two later he heard her moan softly again, flinching a little at the first intimate caress of his tongue, and then there was no sound at all but the thunder of the water around them and his own pounding heartbeat and C.J.'s rapid breathing.

Her fingers tightened convulsively and he could feel her thighs tremble. At that moment, instead of taking her all the way, he straightened, lifting her as he did so that he was standing between her parted thighs. As he slipped deeply into her welcoming warmth she gave a soft cry of pleasure.

He braced her as best he could against the wall of the shower, nearly losing his grip on her when she gave a desperate wriggle, and she grabbed the towel rack to steady herself. It would have been insane to draw it out—not to mention suicidal—so he simply braced his feet as well as he could on the soapy floor and moved strongly and urgently within the circle of her thighs. It took no time at all to carry her over that bright, steep edge and into the shuddering downslope beyond. As her sharp little cries still echoed around them he sank to his knees, carrying her down with him, turned her so she was lying beneath him, legs drawn up in the confines of the etched-glass walls around them, and stopped trying to hang on.

The water pounded down on him and he gave himself over to the primitive power of it, making love to her with a driving, deep urgency that made her moan and buck against him, her body responding strongly again and again, until his whole world just exploded in one heart-stopping uprush that made him shout her name aloud.

It was only long minutes later, panting in C.J.'s arms like a locomotive, that Garrett realized the water hammering down on them was turning distinctly cool. Laughing, he staggered to his feet and helped her up, then turned off the water and pulled the door open to grab a huge fluffy towel and bundle it around her.

"So much for water conservation," he said with a breathless laugh, still panting. "That was insane, C.J. Carruthers. But fantastic. Absolutely... fantastic."

"This can't be normal," she panted back, grinning up at him from the depths of the towel. "We can't be normal, Garrett. I read an article in some magazine not long ago that said the national average for this sort of thing was once a week. We've used up about a month's worth in the past six hours alone!"

"Those once-a-week types obviously don't have a woman like you," he said in a mock growl, holding her face in his hands and kissing her firmly. "Give me a half hour to catch my breath, and I'll see what I can do about using up another week's worth."

"We're already late for breakfast," she reminded him with a slow smile.

"Hell, then we may as well just stay in bed till lunch." Still cradling her face in his hands, he gazed down at her, his heart giving an odd little one-two step that made his breath catch. She was so achingly beautiful he couldn't imagine ever having had any doubts, so perfect in all ways that he felt as though he could step outside and soar. "I want to make you happy, C.J.," he said quietly, realizing with unexpected gentleness that he meant it. "Damn it, lady, I..." *Love you?* It wasn't possible, of course, yet the words had come to him unbidden, had slipped—almost—from his lips.

No lies, he told himself firmly, covering his near miss with another lingering kiss. That's one thing he wouldn't do, was lie to her.

"I am happy," she whispered, turning her face to kiss his palm, and for a moment he thought he saw the glint of unshed tears in her eyes. "We'd better get dressed, Garrett. I'd love to stay in bed with you all day, but I *do* have things to do."

She slipped free of his hands and finished drying herself, thoughtful, slightly remote, and Garrett frowned, having the feeling he was missing something important.

Eight

They did manage, finally, to get down to the main house for breakfast. And although the staff didn't seem to think anything was amiss, C.J. was certain every single one of them knew exactly what she and Garrett had been doing a half hour before.

Bertie, thank heaven, had finished breakfast and was in her office. She'd have taken one look at her, C.J. knew, and would have seen every single telltale clue for exactly what it was.

"This isn't goin' to get to be a habit, is it, this coming in looking for breakfast at this hour?" Cook gave them both a disapproving glance as they wandered into the kitchen. She was dismembering a chicken, the big cleaver flickering in her hand as she worked. "You could've waited an hour and called it lunch."

"See," Garrett murmured, grinning, "I told you we should have—ooph!"

Removing her elbow from his ribs, C.J. smiled at Cook. "Sorry, we got . . . that is, we—"

"Had some business to take care of," Garrett put in, smooth as cream. Had he been a cat, he'd have been licking his whiskers.

"Monkey business, more 'n likely," Cook muttered, eyeing them both shrewdly. "Her Ladyship is lookin' for you, by the way. She's in the sitting room—has company with her she wants you to meet. Though I'd do something about coverin' up that love bite on your neck before you go in, Miss C.J. And *you*," she added with a dark look at Garrett, "had might want to look a little more like a business-type man, and a little less like a tomcat just in from a night of misbehavin'. If you get what I mean."

"All too clearly," Garrett said with a wince.

And C.J., blushing furiously, buttoned her blouse tightly to her throat. "I've never been able to get away with anything in this house," she muttered. "Cook, sometimes I think you know more about this family than we know about ourselves."

"I expect that's so," Cook said contentedly. Then she shot Garrett another penetrating look. "I've known this girl since she was just a little tyke—helped raise her, you might say. So I guess I don't mind telling you that any man who hurts her is going to be sorry." The cleaver came down with a resonating thunk. "*Mighty* sorry."

"I get the picture," Garrett said, hastily backing toward the door.

"Tomcats get that operation to stop them from all that yowlin' and howlin'." She smiled beatifically, and the cleaver fell again, blade glittering. "You have a *real* nice day, now."

C.J. was still laughing as they walked down the corridor toward the sitting room. "You turned the most amazing shade of green, Garrett. I've never seen anyone actually do that before."

"Having a madwoman threaten to emasculate me with a meat cleaver has that effect." He gave a graphic shudder. "It's nothing to joke about, damn it. The woman should be locked up."

"You worry too much. If she didn't use that cleaver on some of the losers Bertie's tried to match me up with over the years, you're safe as houses. Although," she added with a teasing, sidelong look, "you'd probably be smart to keep me happy and uncomplaining."

He grinned. "I'll do my best, Slick. Count on it."

The big formal sitting room, rarely used in these days of less elegant entertaining, ran across the front of the old house, filled with antique Italian furniture and imported Indian rugs and nearly a century's worth of family collectibles and priceless heirlooms. It was flooded with late-morning sunlight, and as she walked in, C.J. tried to look a little less like a woman who's just spent the night with her lover, and a little more like the competent business administrator she was supposed to be.

There were two other people there with Bertie, a distinguished-looking older man with a mane of gray hair and a sailboat tan, and a younger woman who, at first glance, could have been his daughter. C.J. had her mouth open to say something when Garrett breathed a sizzling oath.

"What the *hell* are you two doing here?" He strode by her, face dark with anger.

In that moment, C.J. saw something die in the older man's eyes. Hope, maybe. Certainly the delight that had first blossomed there when they'd come in. He got to his feet almost stiffly.

"I invited them," Bertie said briskly. "Your father called yesterday to ask if you were still here. He told me that he and your...his wife were in Miami, and I invited them over." Bertie's eyes glittered. "C.J., this is Garrett's father, Stafford Jameison, and his wife, Krystal. My grandniece, C.J. Carruthers."

The elder Jameison gripped C.J.'s hand gently and he smiled down at her, his eyes the same tawny gold as his son's but without the fierce anger. Krystal's handshake was firm and warm, and C.J. realized Stafford's new wife wasn't as young as she'd first thought. Nor, she decided thoughtfully, did she look like a Las Vegas stripper. She was beautiful and expensively turned out, and she sat beside her husband looking calm and composed, her hair sedately styled, her figure generous without being flamboyant.

"Garrett, this is neither the time nor the place," his father said quietly, "but we need to talk. I know you're unhappy with my marrying Krystal without telling you first, but—"

"Unhappy?" Garrett wheeled away, his eyes glittering with fury. "Marry who you want. I don't give a damn anymore."

"Garrett!" C.J. stared at him in shock.

"Miss Carruthers, it's all right." Krystal's smile was wry. "Garrett and I have agreed to disagree about my feelings toward his father. He thinks I'm after Stafford's money and—"

"Aren't you?" Garrett faced her challengingly.

"No, I am not." She gazed up at him with weary sadness, eyes searching his. "I don't need his money—or yours. In fact, I signed a prenuptial agreement that guarantees that if your father predeceases me, or if we divorce, I receive absolutely nothing.

"I'm not going to tell you that I've had a perfect past— your private detective has already told you about my ex-husband. And there were other men—not many, but more than I like to think about. I left home when I was fifteen and I've made my own way in the world, and it's been damned rough at times. I've made mistakes. Plenty of them. There are things I wish I could undo, but I can't. I'm no angel, Garrett, but I'm not a bad person. I love your father very much, and I make him happy." She lifted her head almost regally. "And I am not going to apologize for that."

"I accepted Mrs. D'Allaird's invitation because I'd hoped you'd come to terms with our marriage." His father looked at Garrett with the same sad expression. "Obviously you haven't. When you accept Krystal as my wife, and can treat her accordingly, you are welcome in my home, Garrett. Until then, I don't want to see you." He smiled down at his wife, a smile so filled with love and tenderness that it made C.J.'s throat tighten. "I told you I'd try, darling. And I have. Now let's not bore these good people with any more family drama, and go back to Miami, all right?" He turned to Bertie with great dignity. "Thank you, Mrs. D'Allaird. But if you'd be so kind as to call your man Jerome, we would like to leave."

"But I hardly think—" Bertie caught herself, to C.J.'s surprise, and simply nodded. "I'm sorry it turned out like this. I was hoping for something...better." This with a cool look at Garrett, who was standing stone faced and silent to one side.

"If you'll excuse me," he said through gritted teeth, not even looking at his father and Krystal, "I've got work to do." And with that he turned his back on all of them and strode from the room.

"Stubborn young pup," Bertie snapped.

"It's not entirely his fault," his father said with a hint of amusement in his voice. "Since his mother's death, I've been less than...wise in my choice of companions." He grinned suddenly and took Krystal's hand. "Until now."

"And when I met Stafford, I *was* dancing in a Las Vegas nightclub," she put in with a quiet laugh. "If I were Garrett, I'd probably be just as suspicious. I'd just hoped..." Her face lost some of its happiness, and she squeezed her husband's hand, smiling wanly.

They stayed for another few minutes, and when they'd finally gone down to the dock where Jerome had the launch tied, C.J. went looking for Garrett. But he, too, was gone. Winthrup said he'd seen him in shorts and running shoes, sprinting along the beach as though trying to outflank the devil himself, and C.J. went back to work, thoughtful and subdued.

He didn't come back until late that afternoon, and even then he didn't bother looking in on her. She saw him stride past her window, face sullen, and then heard the door to Green Cottage slam closed.

She waited, edgy and restless, trying to keep her mind on foreign-sales options and royalties percentages and not on the fury on Garrett's face as he'd gone storming out that afternoon. But finally she gave up, swearing a little under her breath, and went next door. Her knock echoed away and for a moment or two she thought he wasn't going to answer her. Then she heard a surly, "It's open!" and let herself in.

He was standing by the big window overlooking the gulf, one hand braced on the wall, the other on his hip, his back to the door. He didn't look around as she came in. She contemplated walking across and slipping her arms around him and doing her best to talk him into bed, then thought better of it. He was not, by the look of it, in any kind of romantic mood.

He'd showered and changed into faded jeans but hadn't bothered putting his shirt on yet, and the sunlight pouring through the window glittered on his damp shoulders and hair. "If you're looking for an apology, you've come to the wrong place," he growled. "He had no business coming out here. Not with...her. If he'd wanted to face me down about it, he should have talked to me personally, not gone through Bertie."

C.J. smiled, rubbing her bare arms as she strolled into the room. "Knowing Bertie, I suspect it was more likely the other way around. She has no qualms about meddling in things that are none of her business. And lately she's got this *thing* about family. About tidying up loose ends. She probably figured she'd invite them over, you'd come to your senses and everyone would live happily ever after."

"What she doesn't know about family would fill a book."

"He seems very happy." It was a mistake, saying it out loud like that, but she didn't know any other way.

"For now. Wait six months, when she's cleared out his bank account and redlined his credit cards, and he wakes up one morning to find her—and one of his cars—gone."

"I think you're wrong."

"It's happened before."

"Maybe it's different this time."

"And maybe it's not." He turned to look at her, his eyes hard and a little cool. "Women are like that, Slick. They'll be all sweet and tender until they've got you on the hook, then they'll rip your heart out."

C.J. stiffened, seeing the challenge in his eyes. "Is that what you think I'm planning to do?"

His expression softened slightly, a hint of regret shadowing his eyes. "No," he said hoarsely, turning away to stare out the window again. "No, I don't."

"But you're not sure." C.J. paced across to the fireplace, back again, restless and on edge. "You're having second thoughts, aren't you. About us getting married, I mean."

Garrett's gut pulled tight and he didn't say anything for a long while, and when he did, his voice sounded curiously remote. "I'm starting to wonder if it's a good idea. I'm not—" He shook his head, still refusing to look at her. "I'm no bargain, C.J.," he said quietly, feeling subdued and weary. "If you want the truth, I think you deserve better than I can give you."

"Why don't you let me decide that?"

"Because I'm afraid you'll get hurt, that's why. You think you're in love with me, and that'll get you hurt every time."

"Is that what you're scared of?"

"Scared?" He gave a snort.

"You're scared of me."

"Of you?" He looked around at her again. Knowing, somewhere down deep inside himself, that she was probably right. "How do you figure?"

Her smile widened slightly as she started to walk slowly toward him. Stalking, almost. "You're afraid of falling in love with me. Not just me, I guess—any woman. You see the mistakes your father made, and you think that's what happens when a man trusts. Fall in love, make a fool of yourself, get hurt—isn't that the way it works?"

"More or less." Carefully he started moving away from her, not wanting her too close. She was dangerous, he found himself thinking. She made him want things he knew were impossible, question things he knew to be true. "Love's an illusion. A mirage. It glitters and tempts and promises everything you want, but stays just out of reach. A man can spend his whole life chasing what doesn't exist."

"You're afraid of turning out like your father."

Garrett went very still. "You're way out of line, C.J."

"You're not going to get rid of me this easily."

He took a deep breath, teeth gritted. And said, coolly, calmly, "I don't love you, C.J. Is that plain enough for you?"

He expected her to stare at him in stunned hurt, then wheel away, face crumpling with tears, and bolt from the room. But she didn't. To his surprise, she simply smiled, a cool little smile that made the back of his neck prickle slightly.

"I don't imagine you do," she said conversationally, as though they were talking about their favorite flavor of ice cream. "Love never came into it. It was a business deal, after all. Cut-and-dried and signed on the dotted line. And if you think you're breaking that deal you made with Bertie, you can forget it."

Garrett thought, for one long heartbeat of time, that he'd heard her wrong. Mind spinning a little, he stared at her. "What," he asked hoarsely, "do you mean?"

"Oh, come off it, Garrett," she said impatiently, starting to pace again. "We've both been playing this stupid charade of starry-eyed lovers all week, and you've got to be as sick of it as I am. Let's just be honest with each other for a change."

Like tumblers in a lock, the pieces suddenly fell into place. Garrett was still staring at her, feeling a little numbed somehow. "You know."

"Of course I know," she said even more impatiently. "She's my great-aunt, for crying out loud. Do you think anything goes on in that house that concerns her that I don't know about?"

"How?"

"I've known for weeks that she was up to something, even before I found out about her heart. And then when you turned up, I knew you fit into it somehow." She looked across the room at him, eyes unreadable in the shadows where she was standing. "I went through her files until I found the contract."

Garrett's stomach roiled, thinking of her reading those sterile, cold lines of print, remembering the clauses, the trade-offs. He thought, too, of the past couple of weeks, all the lies and the posturing and the playacting... and all the while, she'd known. Every word, every smile, every sweet, long upswept look, every touch—they'd all been meaningless.

And he'd started to believe, he thought savagely. He'd actually let himself start to *believe!* "Nice," he said drolly. "Does she know you go through her business files when her back's turned?"

She laughed. "Strange, isn't it, how another person's lack of ethics is so much worse than our own. Where Bertie's welfare is at stake, Garrett, I'll stoop to anything. Even marrying you."

Bull's-eye. It hit home with a marksman's accuracy, and he flinched, feeling himself flush. "So these past two weeks have just been a waste of time."

Something shifted deep in her eyes, and a flash of red stained her cheeks. "I guess that depends on what you define as a waste. I got the impression you were enjoying yourself."

Another hit. Her aim was deadly. "I was," he drawled. "And you?"

That got her. The red flared to crimson and she turned away, but not before he saw the hurt in her eyes. Her back stayed ramrod straight, though, and he could see her taking a deep breath, as though bracing herself for another exchange.

"I don't know if 'enjoy' is the right word. It wasn't half as distasteful as it could have been. I guess I should thank you for that." She looked over her shoulder at him, eyes touchingly defiant. "The hard part was making sure you thought it was all your idea. That *was* a condition of the contract, wasn't it? That I fell in love with you? Wooed and won, I think was the rather quaint terminology. Bertie's idea, of course—only she'd think of something as heroic and endearing.'"

He stared at her. "God, you're cold."

"When I have to be," she said with steel in her voice.

It was his turn to take a deep, calming breath. He ran his fingers through his hair, feeling suddenly worn out, not really giving a damn. "What happens now?"

"Nothing changes. We pretend we're in love, we get married, we stay out of each other's way as much as possible. We can write up another contract, if you like—our own this time—specifying things like the fact that I promise to continue sleeping with you, and that I'll have kids and so on. As far as the world knows, we'll be just another happily married couple. Only you and I have to know the truth."

"Did I say cold? You'd freeze rock."

"And I suppose you agreed to marry me out of a genuine concern for my welfare and happiness—the multimillion-dollar business arrangement you and Bertie put together had nothing to do with it."

Another hit, dead center. Eyes narrowing, Garrett looked at her for a long while, trying to equate this C.J. Carruthers with the one he *thought* he knew. "I think I underestimated you," he said softly. "I think we all did."

"That's the problem with everyone in this damned house," she said with an edging of anger in her voice. "You all underestimate me. You see what you want to see, and never bother looking any deeper. No one thinks I've got what it takes." She lifted her head slightly and stared across the room at him, her expression cool and very, very determined. "Well, I've got news for you. I *do* have what it takes. I'm not overjoyed at the prospect of marrying you, but it's what Bertie wants—and you thought it was a good idea once, obviously. Since I'm the one with the most to lose, I figure it's my call. And I say we're going through with it."

"And if I refuse?"

"You won't. You gave Bertie your word. And from what I hear, that means something."

He winced. "You know how to hit where it hurts, don't you."

"I do what I have to," she said roughly. "Bertie took me in when no one else wanted me. She gave me a home, she gave me love, she gave me everything a child could want or need. The least I can do for her now is give her the peace of mind she wants by marrying you. She's terrified she's going to die and leave me unprotected and uncared for and— But you know all this. You wouldn't have signed that contract without knowing all the details first."

Garrett found himself shaking his head slowly. "Boy, you're something else. You make Krystal look like a Girl Scout. You've been playing me like a prize trout right from the beginning."

"It's what you wanted, isn't it?"

"I thought you were different," he grated, knowing it shouldn't make any difference. That in a way he should be *glad* it was all out in the open, that he didn't have to lie anymore, didn't have to pretend to feel the love that wasn't there. And yet, for some reason, it made him feel chilled and old and alone. "But you're like all the others," he whispered. "You say whatever you have to say to get what you want. Do whatever you need to do. Make a man believe that—" He bit it off, taking a deep, angry breath. "Hell, I should have known you'd be no different."

"Garrett, I—" She paused, as though wanting to say something and not knowing the words, her eyes searching his intently. "I never lied to you," she finally said, very softly. "When we made love last night, it wasn't some kind of trick. I . . . I admit that I hurried things along a bit, but only because I was trying to make it easier for you. I—"

She looked away, her cheeks suddenly pink. "I didn't know how you felt about making love to me. You *seemed* sincere enough, but I had no idea how much was real and how much was just good acting. And I thought if I just . . . *made* things happen, without either of us having to think about it too much, it would just be one less thing to . . . worry about."

Garrett swore, rubbing his eyes wearily. How much *had* just been good acting, he found himself wondering. Damned little, he suspected. He'd responded to her last night like any man does to a beautiful and desirable woman, wanting her with every cell of his being, delighting in her, enjoying her. *Loving* her. For those long hours, he'd stopped the games, the pretending. They'd been real last night, the two of them—as real as any man and woman lost in the magic of each other.

Maybe that's why it hurt so damned much to now discover that it hadn't been real. That, in the end, he'd been beguiled, after all.

"It changes things," he said finally.

"All it changes is the fact that you can now stop pretending to feel things for me that you don't feel." She sounded as tired as he felt, her voice dispirited and empty. "And the fact, I guess, that we both have to admit we're not really very nice people. You were willing to use me, but no more than I was willing to be used. I don't know what that makes us, but I have a feeling I'd rather not know."

"Yeah," Garrett said in a soft, harsh voice, knowing—all too well—what she meant. "Yeah, you're probably right."

"But I do think that it would be a good idea if we—" She stopped and looked out the window, frowning, and Garrett turned to see what had caught her attention.

There was nothing out there but the silky waters of the gulf, then he heard someone shouting in the distance and, even more faintly, the unmistakable thump of a big helicopter coming in low and fast. And then, suddenly, Cook raced by the window, looking disheveled and panic-stricken, and a moment later she was pounding on the cottage door.

C.J. was already there, pulling it open, and Cook stumbled in. "It's your great-aunt," she wailed, bursting into tears. "It's Bertie! She . . . she's had a heart attack!"

She didn't even have time to cry until later.

It had all seemed impossible—a nightmare in slow motion. The air ambulance had been landing on the front lawn even as she'd hit the door of the house at a dead run. The turmoil from the big rotors was tearing up the gardens and sending up small tornadoes of leaves and grass cuttings and bruised, torn flowers, and C.J.'s first inane thought had been that Bertie was going to be raising merry hell about *that*.

Then there had been the trip across to the hospital in Fort Myers, then the one a few hours later to Miami, and all she remembered about it was Winthrup's gray, haggard face and Garrett being everywhere at once, snapping out orders like a battlefield general until he got things the way he wanted them.

And the sitting. That she could remember, sitting there helpless and numb with fear for hour after endless hour, drinking machine coffee without even tasting it, aware of Winthrup and Garrett talking to her now and again but having no idea of what they said, of what her replies had been. Knowing nothing but the encompassing terror that someone was going to come in at any minute and tell her that Bertie was gone.

But it was only hours later, after the worst panic was over and word had finally come down that Bertie's condition was guarded but good, that expectations were positive, that C.J. realized it had all been real. She awoke without even being aware of having fallen asleep, and found herself lying under a blanket on an acre of bed in what she thought at first was a luxury hotel.

It was only when she got up, groggy and disoriented, and started wandering around that she realized it was no hotel, but a beachfront penthouse condo with a million-dollar view. And then she vaguely remembered arguing with Garrett about where she'd stay, and him simply taking charge of that, too....

There was hot coffee in the vast high-tech kitchen and a big platter of assorted sliced fruit under protective plastic wrap, and, beside it, a portable phone with a note propped against it.

Bertie's okay, it said in Garrett's untidy scrawl. *Prognosis good. I'm taking Winthrup over to hospital now, will be back pronto. Make yourself at home.* The hospital phone number was underneath, with the name of the person to talk to if she wanted a prompt report on Bertie's condition without having to go through normal channels.

The woman at the other end was courteous and efficient and could answer all her questions, and C.J. hung up the phone a few minutes later feeling infinitely better. There was no point in going back to the hospital yet—Bertie was resting, no one was allowed in to see her, and if her condition changed at all, someone would call. C.J. wandered around for a few minutes more, feeling jumpy and at loose ends, then decided to take Garrett at his word.

She found the same bedroom again after a couple of false starts, and discovered that someone—Garrett, probably— had brought over a suitcase full of toiletries and fresh clothing. Taking the phone with her in case the hospital called, she filled the tub to the brim with steaming hot water and soaked away some of her fright, and when she finally dragged herself out and got dressed and staggered back to the kitchen for more coffee, she actually felt almost calm.

She had just combed her soaking-wet hair back from her face with her fingers and was pouring herself a generous mug full of the hot, fragrant coffee when she realized she was no longer alone. There was a set of car keys lying on the counter with a folded-up newspaper beside them, and it was then that she noticed the tie hanging from a convenient doorknob, and the dark suit jacket tossed just as casually over a nearby chair.

He was in the massive white-on-white living room, sitting on one of the big sprawling leather sofas with his long legs stretched out, head resting on the cushioned back, eyes closed.

She thought he was asleep at first, but he opened his eyes and looked at her, managing a weary smile. "How are you doing?"

"Okay. Would you like some coffee?"

"Yeah. Thanks."

He looked like hell. He hadn't shaved in who knew how long and his cheeks were dark with stubble, his hair in tangled disarray, his usually crisp shirt wilted and wrinkled. He'd unbuttoned it, maybe planning to take it off before exhaustion had ambushed him, and it gaped widely, exposing a broad expanse of flat sun-browned chest and belly.

"Is this your place?" She handed him the cup and he took it with a grateful smile.

"Yeah." The smile faded as though it was too great an effort to keep it on his mouth. "You wanted me to get you a hotel room close to the hospital, but it was just as easy to bring you back here. You don't remember the drive over?"

C.J. shook her head and sat down across from him, cradling the mug of coffee. "I guess I was pretty out of it."

"Asleep was more like it. I carried you up from the car and put you to bed."

C.J. nodded, staring into the steaming coffee, then up at him. "Thanks, Garrett. For getting Bertie transferred here, for getting the specialists, for...everything. I wasn't tracking too well...."

"You were tracking just fine," he said quietly. "You were in control of things right from the start—I just stayed out of your way and did what I could."

C.J. smiled slightly. "That's not the way I remember it, but thanks." She looked at him for a moment. "Why don't you have a shower, then get some sleep—you look terrible."

"Yeah," he said with a sigh, "maybe I will. I'm bushed." He pushed himself upright and braced his elbows on his thighs, rubbing his face with his hand. "I'll grab a couple hours' sleep, then we can head back to the hospital. They said we could see her about three this afternoon if all goes well."

"Is Winthrup with her?"

Garrett nodded. "I offered to put him up here but he refuses to leave her."

"I have to make some phone calls—do Bertram and the boys know yet?"

"I thought I'd let you call them." Garrett paused delicately. "When you're up to it, we're going to have to talk about . . . things."

"About where and how you fit into PI now, you mean," she said calmly. "As far as I'm concerned, nothing changes—you're still taking over for Emmett. I don't know if you realize this or not, but I have power of attorney. So as long as Bertie is ill, I'm effectively in charge of damned near everything."

He just nodded. "I probably don't have to tell you that your great-uncle is going to come down here and try to bully you into turning the reins over to him—ostensibly until Bert's on her feet. And once he's got his foot in the door, he—"

"He's not going to get his foot in the door." C.J. felt oddly calm and in control, and wondered how long it was going to last. "I have a contingent of lawyers to back me up if James decides to argue. I doubt he'll go that far though, not at first. He'll try reason, then compassionate concern, then exasperation. And when those don't work, he'll try to intimidate me by pointing out that I can't possibly understand the implications of what I'm doing, and that if I insist on being pigheaded and silly about it, I'm jeopardizing the very foundations of PI."

"And when that doesn't work?"

"He'll bring in a team of attorneys to try and prove that Bertie's no longer competent and that PI's best interests cannot be served by allowing a young, inexperienced girl—me—to control fifty-one percent of the voting shares."

"I have the feeling," Garrett said slowly, "that great-uncle James is going to be in for a very unpleasant surprise."

C.J. simply nodded, staring into the coffee mug. Then, taking another deep breath, she looked up and met Garrett's gaze evenly. "One more reason," she said simply, "that I want us to get married as quickly as possible."

Nine

——

"Married?" Garrett straightened slowly. "You mean you still want to go through with it? Even now?"

"Especially now." She got to her feet and walked across to the wall of glass overlooking the beach and ocean. Far below, long, lazy whitecaps swept up onto sand the color of crushed opals, the deep blue water farther out confettied with hundreds of sailboats. "Not for myself, or even for you, but for Bertie. She wants me married before she dies—well, she's going to see me married."

"Damn it, C.J...." She could hear him swear softly under his breath, then heard the click of the mug onto the glass coffee table and braced herself slightly. He moved silently on the thick cream-colored carpeting, until he stood just behind her, not touching but so close she could feel the heat radiating off his bare chest. "I know you think you're doing the right thing, C.J., but I'm not sure you know what—"

"I know exactly what I'm doing." Carefully she stepped away from him. "You gave your word, Garrett. You signed a contract. And you *are* going to honor it."

He swore again, the words pungent and edged with anger. "Fine. You want to get married, then we'll damned well get married. A friend of mine's a judge—I'll call him this afternoon and set it up."

He reached out suddenly and grasped her upper arm and swung her toward him, his face hard and remote. "But only on one condition, Slick. I don't want you falling in love with me and changing all the rules a year down the road. When all is said and done, this is just a business deal. No love, no romance, no hearts and flowers. I promised your great-aunt I'll be the best husband I can manage to be, and I meant it. But I'm the man I am, C.J., no more, no less. I'm not going to change. Fall in love with me, and you're going to get hurt, understand?"

"Yes," she whispered. Except it was already too late. . . .

"And no sleeping in the spare room, either—marry me, and you damned well sleep with me. I'll do the best I can by you, C.J., but you're going to have to meet me halfway. This marriage is going to be for real, or it isn't going to be, is that clear?"

"Yes," she whispered again, wondering how in God's name he thought that just saying the words would make it so.

The pressure of his fingers on her arm lessened slightly and he gazed down at her searchingly. "Tell me one thing," he said thickly. "Just tell me why you'd go through with it now. Knowing I don't love you. Knowing it was all just a . . . setup."

Because I love you and this is as close as I'll come to having you love me, she felt like telling him. "Because the day finally comes when you have to grow up and put your dreams away," she said flatly. "This is real life, Garrett. Something I haven't had a lot of experience with. That's why Bertie hired you to marry me, because she's afraid I can't cope with real life.''

"I think you could cope with anything life throws at you." He said it honestly, with admiration in his eyes.

C.J. smiled humorlessly and turned to look out at the sailboats again. "I was the original fairy-tale princess, growing up on my own enchanted island. I was safe there. Protected. I didn't even go to real school—we had a live-in tutor until I was in my teens. There were no other kids to play with, and I grew up surrounded by Bertie and her weird and wonderful friends, thinking I was normal in spite of the fact that everyone around me was fifty years my senior. And the best part was that no one treated me like a kid—they all treated me as though I were just a small adult. Within reason, I mean.''

"Sounds like every kid's idea of heaven."

"It was Paradise." She smiled slightly at the old joke. "And you're right—I loved it. I didn't even *like* kids my age. I thought they were dull and silly, and I hated going off the island. Then Bertie decided I needed some acclimatizing with younger people and sent me to private school on the mainland for a year."

"Which you hated."

C.J. had to laugh. "Boy, did I hate it! The other girls were like an alien species to me. It was as though they had their own secret little society and I was on the outside, not knowing the language, the rituals, the...*code*." She gazed out the window for a long while. "That was the loneliest year of my life. They never accepted me. Although who could blame them—I was this really strange kid who could discuss Sartre and Camus and world politics in the same breath. I was reading Dante when they were reading Nancy Drew, and listening to Mozart while they were discovering the latest rock band. I finally wrote to Bertie and told her how miserable I was, and a couple weeks later she took me home. And I stayed there until I left for college."

"That must have been rough, too."

"Not really. Oh, I was still a little weird, I guess, but I'd also learned how to fit in by then. And Bertie and I had done a lot of traveling, so I wasn't quite the bumpkin you'd expect. Besides, there were enough other overly serious people on campus that I didn't stand out like I did when I was ten."

Garrett laughed, the first real laugh she'd heard in two days, and it made her heart give a little twist. "But I was glad when I was finally back on Paradise for good," she said quietly. "It's . . . peaceful there. I knew, logically, that it couldn't last forever, but it . . . oh, I don't know. It's always seemed enchanted, I guess. As though time doesn't mean the same thing there. As though Bertie and Winthrup and the others were ageless, as though we could just go on the way we were forever."

He didn't say anything, but she knew he was thinking the same thing she was . . . that time had finally caught up to them just as it did to everyone else.

"So," she said crisply, shaking off the past, "the time has come for me to join the real world. Bertie seems to have made it this time, but there will be next times, I see that now. And sooner or later she won't make it back, and that's just the way it is. I want her to live forever because I can't imagine a world without her in it, but I know that's not going to happen. She wants me married and happy before she goes— I intend to fulfill that dream. And maybe, with luck, I can give her a grandchild or two to spoil."

"And you?" He asked it softly, and she knew he was watching her. "I know why you're doing it for Bertie, but what do *you* get out of it?"

C.J. smiled slightly and turned to look at him, her gaze holding his. "I want just what I'm going to get, Garrett. Absolutely nothing." And, with that, she turned and walked out of the room.

It was a lie, of course. She wanted it all—his love, his friendship, his warmth, his laughter. She wanted to look across a room and see him there and know his loving smile was for her. Wanted to wake in the night and hear his heart beating against hers and know that even in sleep he dreamed of her. Wanted everything she could never have.

But she'd take what she could get.

It was a cop-out in a way, she knew that. Making Bertie happy was only a part of it. Down deep, there was the fear—a little girl's fear of waking alone and knowing no one was there. Of being abandoned. Of having nowhere to go, no one to take her in and comfort her and tell her it was going to be all right.

If life were *fair*, no child would go to bed loved one night and awaken an orphan. If life were *fair*, she'd have grown up with parents like everyone else, maybe even with brothers and sisters and a cat and some dogs and a big backyard with swings, and love enough for everyone.

If life were fair, Lord Jamie Kildonan would come riding out of the mists and sweep her up onto his saddle bow and ride off with her and they'd spend eternity together, madly in love.

But life wasn't fair. Four-year-old girls did wake up abandoned and unwanted, and dark-eyed pirates didn't just appear from nowhere to fulfill a lonely woman's fantasies. So she'd settle for marrying Garrett Jameison instead. And damned well make the best of it, as she had with everything else in her life.

If he was half as smart as people kept telling him he was, Garrett was still advising himself a few hours later, he'd call in the best lawyers he could find and get himself out of that damned contract of Bertie's. It wouldn't be that difficult—after all, what woman in her right mind would trade her grandniece for a piece of corporate pie?

Except there were a couple of problems with that. First, he'd given his word, as C.J. had all too clearly reminded him. And second, he was also starting to realize he didn't really want to get out of it.

Sure, it was crazy. Sure, he'd spent most of the past two and a half weeks alternately complimenting himself on his inherent cleverness and calling himself six kinds of a fool. And sure, he was probably going to spend a lot of time over the rest of his life regretting it. But when you added it all up and cut right to the bottom line, it still made a kind of perverse sense to marry the woman.

And that's why, three days later, in a small civil ceremony attended by exactly four people including the judge, Garrett David Jameison married Chastity Jane Carruthers and changed his life forever.

It was a strange little ceremony, with he and C.J. as stone faced as statues, and Winthrup fluttering around like a worried aunt, and the judge looking more and more bemused by the passing minute.

They decided to keep it quiet, at least until Bertie was stronger, and after the blessedly brief ceremony, Winthrup and C.J. went back up to the hospital, and Garrett, feeling decidedly strange, headed down to his sorely neglected offices to get caught up on some work.

It was hours later that he headed back to his condo, realizing as he gave the keys to his car to the garage attendant that this was his wedding day and he hadn't passed more than two dozen words with his new bride, including the all-important "I do." Didn't even know, as a matter of fact, if she was here or not. Didn't know if she was going to spend her wedding night here with him, or back on Paradise, advising the staff there of her new marital status and picking up some of her clothes.

And so when he unlocked the door to his home and walked in to the unmistakable scent of roasting chicken, he didn't honestly know if he was relieved or annoyed.

She was in the kitchen, still wearing the understated but wonderfully elegant white suit she'd worn to the ceremony, although she'd kicked off her pumps and was padding around barefoot, frowning as she peered into one of the wall ovens.

"Hi, honey, I'm home!"

She wheeled around as though shot and stared at him in startled consternation, and Garrett gave a rueful chuckle. "Sorry. I was just trying to lighten things up a little."

"Oh."

She looked more scared than amused, Garrett thought. And found himself, very suddenly, almost feeling sorry for her. "Relax, C.J.," he teased gently. "This is as new to me as it is to you. We'll just blunder around until we get the hang of it, and in a few years we'll be laughing about it."

She nodded, looking thoroughly skeptical, and he sighed inwardly and gestured around the kitchen. "Find everything okay?"

She nodded again.

Trying to put her at ease, he wandered over to the wall oven and looked through the glass door. "I forgot to ask you if you can cook."

"You forgot to ask me a lot of things," she said, making an effort to smile. It wasn't very successful. "I, um, didn't know if you wanted to eat in or go out, so I took a chance you'd be tired and want to stay home." She swallowed, twisting the corner of a tea towel between her fingers.

"I was going to go shopping, but I didn't know where the nearest market was, and without a car..." She shrugged, looking cornered and miserable. "Anyway, I found a couple of game hens in the freezer and did the best I could. And the security manager for the building dropped by and said you're to call him about...me. I told him I was your—that we were married, but he obviously didn't believe me. That's another reason I didn't go shopping. I was afraid if I went out they wouldn't let me back in."

"Damn." Garrett raked his hair back with his hand. "I should have taken care of that, I'm sorry. I'll straighten things out and get you a coded access card for the building and parking area. I'll take you in to the bank tomorrow and introduce you to the manager, and we'll open a joint account. And I'd better have my secretary start calling around to get you on my credit cards, too. And my attorney— damn, I'll call him first thing in the morning. If I get hit by a bus tomorrow, it'll come as a nasty shock to a lot of people to find I'm married." *Married*. The word still jarred him.

"I'd better call my attorney, too," she said quietly. "He should know you're my...that we're—that I'm married. In case *I'm* the one who gets hit by the bus."

Garrett gave a snort of humorless laughter. "I didn't realize getting married was so complicated. The only experience I've had with the institution is trying to get my dad *out* of it a couple of times without losing his shirt."

"I'll have to get my driver's license and social security card and so on changed...we never did discuss names, did we."

"Names?"

"Well...my name. Do you prefer me to keep my maiden name, or take yours?"

"Honey, until today I didn't even know what the 'C.J.' stood for." He tried to make it into a joke, but neither of them were laughing. "Damn," he said again, putting more feeling into it this time. "C.J....hell, this is harder than I thought it was going to be. We're just..." He walked across to her, hating the way she flinched slightly as he put his hands gently on her shoulders. "Honey, if this is going to work, we're just going to have to take it slow and easy, okay? One step at a time."

She nodded again, still not looking convinced, and to his surprise he found himself bending down and kissing her gently on the cheek. She smelled of lavender soap and sage and for a split second he contemplated turning the oven off and picking her up in his arms and taking her into the bedroom and making love to her. But she stiffened very slightly and he backed off instead, swearing savagely at himself for thinking it could ever be that easy.

They ate by candlelight, a tense, silent meal that only magnified the uneasiness between them until it sang through the room like wind through high-tension wires. It would get easier, C.J. told herself with forced calm, unable to even look at him—her new husband—across the wide, glass-topped table. They were just awkward with the newness of it, each glance and word and gesture strange and unfamiliar and fraught with misunderstanding.

And, too, there was the unspoken awareness between them that, sooner or later, they were going to have to go to bed. Oddly enough, it probably would have been easier to face had they not already been there. The memory of that long and wondrous night of lovemaking and tenderness and laughter hung between them like a tangible thing, adding nuances of intimacy neither of them wanted, remembrances of a closeness that could never be recaptured.

They cleared up the dishes together, being scrupulous not to touch or even look at each other as they wandered around the big kitchen, looking for things to do. Garrett finally excused himself and went into the dark-paneled retreat that was his den and office, muttering something about having some calls to make. And C.J., feeling lost and at loose ends, drifted through the large, unfamiliar rooms without aim or purpose, realizing, with a thickness in her throat, that this was where she was going to be living now. That this was home.

She found herself staring out at the twinkling lights of Miami, crying silently, and wondered how it was possible to feel so alone and empty. She wanted Bertie, she thought in silent desperation. She wanted Bertie and Winthrup and Bertie's pack of small savage dogs and Cook and the laughter and warmth, wanted it all the way it had always been, unchanged and forever.

And finally, knowing it couldn't be postponed any longer, she walked down to the huge master bedroom and got ready for bed. She took a long hot bath, then brushed her hair until it shone and pulled on the creamy white negligee she'd bought two days ago, with its froth of silk ruffles around the shoulders, and stood staring at her reflection in the bathroom mirror.

Not how you dreamed it would be, is it? she asked the pale, frightened-looking woman in the mirror. Your wedding night was supposed to be special and wonderful and magical, a covenant between you and your new husband and the love you share....

Carefully she let her gaze slip from that of the woman in the mirror, not liking what she saw there. And, as carefully, she pushed the dreams as far back in her mind as possible. She'd given her word. And she would not go back on it.

The silken sheets on Garrett's huge bed were cool and fresh scented and she lay there in the darkness and silence, listening to the sough of the air-conditioning and the thumping of her own heart. She felt cold and alone and a little unfocused, as though this whole thing were just a bad dream. Paradise, she thought with an aching desperation. She'd wake up on Paradise and find none of it had been real....

She must have dozed, because the next thing she realized was that the bedside lamp was on and Garrett was standing there staring down at her with a peculiar expression on his face, half surprise and half annoyance, as though finding her in his bed was the *last* thing he'd expected—or wanted.

But he didn't say anything, just frowned a little as he turned away and started to undress, pulling off his watch and placing it on the bureau, then tugging his shirt out of his slacks and unbuttoning it and tossing it over the back of a convenient chair on his way into the bathroom.

He was in there for what seemed a long, long while, and when he came out he didn't even look at her, pausing to toss his slacks onto the chair with the shirt, then walking across to the bed. To her immense relief, he'd kept his briefs on, and then, to her equally immense discomfort, he started to strip them off as he reached the bed.

She kept her eyes averted, knowing her cheeks were turning a vivid shade of crimson, and wondered what the new groom would do if his bride burst into tears and bolted out of the room. But before she could find out, Garrett tossed one corner of the sheet back, flicked off the bedside lamp and slipped into bed beside her.

She was relieved when he didn't turn to her immediately, or even try to touch her, and she lay and listened to him breathing in the darkness beside her, wondering if he could hear her heart pounding. Time seemed to stretch forever, as elastic as warm taffy, each thud of her heart echoing the seconds as they ticked by. And finally she heard him swear softly and fervently under his breath and he rolled toward her, one hand slipping around her shoulder, the other resting on the pillow beside her head. He lifted himself up on one elbow and gazed down at her for a thoughtful minute, then lowered his mouth to hers and kissed her gently.

She pretended to respond, sighing with what she hoped sounded like real passion, running her hand down his hard-muscled back and trying desperately to remember what it had been like making love with him before, hoping to re-kindle some of that need and desire just on the memory alone. Murmuring what she thought was a fair imitation of the love words she'd heard him use the night they were together, she let her hand drift down his back and around to the blade of his hipbone, then—teeth gritted—down the slab of his belly.

He swore again, sounding tired and angry, and caught her wrist before she could touch him. "Don't," he said roughly.

Feeling another hot blush sweep across her cheeks, C.J. swallowed. "Sorry," she whispered. "I thought—"

"This isn't going to work." He rolled away from her, almost pushing her from him, and lay on his back in the shadowed night. "I don't want it like this. I don't want *you* like this."

"But I thought you wanted—"

"More than a fake moan or two and a quick grope under the sheets," he said with quiet savagery.

It stung to the quick and she could feel her eyes filling with tears. "I'm sorry," she whispered, fighting to keep the sob out of her voice. "I—I'm just nervous and—"

"You can't stand the thought of having me even touch you."

"Garrett, that's not—"

Swearing ferociously, he sat up and swung his legs over the side of the bed. "I don't know why the hell I let myself think that we—" He caught whatever he'd been about to say, swearing again as he raked his fingers through his hair, not looking at her. "Let's just write tonight off as a bad idea and get some sleep, okay? You'll probably be more comfortable in the spare room. And there's a lock on the door, so you—"

"A *lock* on the door?" C.J. turned her head to look at him, seeing nothing but a wall of muscled back. "Why would I need to lock the door, for crying out loud—you can't get rid of me fast enough. Or is it to keep me *in?*"

"Come off it, C.J.," he growled. "You know what I mean." It was all starting to unravel, Garrett thought despairingly. He'd handled it all wrong, and now things were just going from bad to worse and—

"No, as a matter of fact," she said with crisp precision, "I do not. You made it patently clear that if we got married I'd be expected to sleep with you. I took that to mean we'd

be doing more than just *sleeping*. I took it to mean
we'd—''

"I *know* what you took it to mean." His voice rose
slightly.

"So that night we spent together, that night I came to
your cottage, was just ... acting."

"If you believe that," he grated, "you don't know a
damned thing about men—and even less about me." He
thought of that night, taunting himself with the images of
her lying in his arms, head thrown back, teeth caught across
her lower lip to bite back a moan of delighted satisfaction
as he'd eased himself into her, the feel of her lithe, strong
body moving helplessly under his and the way she'd clamped
her thighs on his hips when—

He swore again, vividly and angrily, and felt her shrink
away from him. "This doesn't have anything to do with that
night. Things have changed, that's all."

She was silent for a moment or two. "What do you
mean?"

"I mean," he said through gritted teeth, "that this whole
thing leaves a bad taste in my mouth. I feel as though...hell,
I don't know. A man likes to think a woman's in his bed
because she *wants* to be, not because she *has* to be."

There was another long silence. "We are married," she
said a bit primly. "You said this had to be a part of it, and
I agreed."

"You make it sound as much fun as a tax audit."

"It's not as though it's the first time," she went on in that
dry, precise voice.

"I *know* it's not the first time," he bellowed. "Damn it,
I was *there* the first time, remember?"

"You don't have to be rude," she said coolly. "Are you
going to make love to me or not?"

He thought about it for a long moment. Thought about
just turning to her and damned well doing it, as much to
shut her up as anything. Quick, tidy, almost clinical ... just

his husbandly duty. They hadn't gotten into this marriage for the romance, right?

Except, if he did, it would destroy any chance they had of finding even a little bit of happiness together. And a lifetime was a long time to spend with a woman who hated your guts.

"No," he said wearily, rubbing his eyes with the heels of his hands, elbows on knees. "No, C.J., I'm not going to make love *to* you—tonight, or any night. Married or not, that comes just a little too close to outright rape for my tastes. So I'll wait until you're ready to make love *with* me."

"I didn't realize I'd married a romantic." But there was, to Garrett's relief, the slightest bit of humor in the words, a hint of thawing. He felt her sit up, sighing, and then, after what seemed like a long while, she touched his shoulder, just a fleeting, gentle brush of fingertips. "Thanks, Garrett," she whispered. "And I'm sorry. I—"

"Don't say it, C.J.," he told her roughly. "I want you, damn it—so bad I feel like my insides are on fire. But not like that. Not as part of some deal, just a physical mating that doesn't mean a damned thing." And yet, he asked himself brutally, he didn't love her, so just how much *meaning* could he expect?

The bed rocked slightly as she slipped from between the sheets. He knew she was standing by the bed uncertainly, looking at him, waiting for some sign that he wanted her to stay or go, but he kept his back to her, refusing to make it easy for her.

"Good night, then," she whispered, her voice curiously thick. "I'll see you in the morning."

"Yeah." He rubbed his stubbled face tiredly, shoulders slumping as he heard the bedroom door close softly behind her. "Yeah, I'll see you in the morning," he whispered to no one.

He must have, finally, fallen asleep, because he dreamed of making love to her. In his dream she came slipping back into his bed, all naked satin skin and soft laughter, her mouth seeking his, hands caressing, teasing, guiding. Then something awakened him with a jolt and he swore groggily and peered into the darkness, wondering—when he saw her standing by the bed—if this was just another part of the same dream.

If it was, it was damned real. Her cheeks were silvered with tears and she was shivering so badly he could see the tremors run through her in spasm after spasm, and finally, still a little dazed with sleep, he realized she really was there. Without saying anything, he lifted the sheet for her and after a moment she slipped under it and into his arms, shaking so hard he could hear her teeth chattering.

"I know y-you d-don't w-w-want me here," she stammered, giving another convulsive shiver, "but c-c-could you j-just hold me?" And then she burst into tears.

He held her awkwardly, not knowing what to do, listening to the long, ragged sobs tear through her. It was like holding on to a block of carved ice and he tugged her into the curve of his body as best he could and started rubbing her back, wrapping her icy legs and feet with his.

"I'm s-so s-s-scared," she sobbed into his throat. "If I lose B-Bertie, I've g-got no one! She's all I've g-got!"

"You've got me," he murmured against her ear, hugging her tightly against him. "You'll always have me, C.J."

The harsh sobs let up after a while, turning into soft little hiccups, and he realized a little bit later that she'd fallen asleep. Had never, he suspected, been entirely awake. She'd probably had a nightmare and had come wandering in looking for comfort without even being fully aware of what she was doing.

Which probably meant there'd be hell to pay in the morning, he decided wearily. But the fact was that she fit in against him just about perfectly, and it was easier to leave her there than to carry her back to the spare room without waking her up, which would mean trying to explain what she was doing in his bed, which would probably lead to yet another argument.

He was almost asleep when he felt her stir, sighing deeply, and he braced himself slightly for an explosion that never came. She seemed to be tangled up in that wisp of froth she called a nightgown and gave a wriggle to get more comfortable, coming to rest tucked even more intimately against him. Her legs were still tangled with his, one thigh tucked up between his, and he wondered if she was really awake or just dreaming again.

He didn't actually know what made him realize that she wasn't asleep. A subtle change in her breathing, maybe, or the way she shivered lightly when he ran his hand down her back, not with cold this time but with something else all together. Even the weight of her in his arms felt suddenly different, no longer a burden but something supple and warm and alive.

He stroked the long, smooth curve of her back again and she arched and moved against him with a little purring sound of pleasure, the muscles in her thigh tightening and relaxing, her breath warm on his collarbone. He shifted slightly and turned her so her mouth was under his and her lips parted with welcome and she sighed again, her fingertips brushing his cheek.

He stopped thinking about it after the first few cautious minutes and simply let himself fall into the sleepy pleasure of having her there, deciding that even if she didn't want to make love, a little shared closeness wouldn't hurt either of them. At each step, he briefly considered stopping it before it got away from them and sending her back to the spare room, but then she'd move just so, or touch him there, and his good intentions would get scattered all to hell and he'd have to start over again.

But finally it got to the point where she was naked, although he couldn't remember if he'd shucked her out of the nightgown or if she'd wriggled out of it herself, and she was moving against him and murmuring in a caught, urgent little voice, her caresses becoming more and more explicit. And then he was stroking her lower belly and then her inner thighs and then he was touching her, parting her, and as her body enfolded his questing fingers like hot liquid silk, she gave a breathless little cry.

"If you...want me...to...stop," Garrett panted against her mouth, "say so...."

"Now?" Laughter bubbled through the one word, breathless and warm. "Are you serious?"

"Deadly," he got out between clenched teeth. "Because it's now or never, sweetheart...."

"Never," she whispered against his mouth, wrapping her arms around his neck and lifting her hips against his hand. "Oh, please...never...!"

And so he didn't stop, and a few minutes later he forgot even asking the question as he slipped his hands under the firm curve of her bottom and lifted her and she moaned in pleasure at that breath-stopping moment when flesh cleaves flesh cleanly and sweetly, and then there was no stopping at all.

Ten

"**P**ig's ears!" Bertie's beady black eyes glittered. "Why in heaven's name would I want to marry Winthrup? I just came close to dying, not losing my mind!"

"Bertie, it's time you let him make an honest woman of you," C.J. said calmly. Or as calm as it was possible to be with teeth gritted and fists clenched. "You've had him on a string for twenty years, and it's not fair."

Bertie gave a snort and patted her hair, then tugged the peach silk bed jacket more closely around her shoulders. "I'm too old to get married."

"*Winthrup's* too old," C.J. said impatiently. "Too old to be sneaking up to your bedroom at night like some kid with a hormone overload. It's not . . . dignified. And it's dangerous, to boot, having him tottering up and down those stairs in the dark."

"Winthrup," Bertie said indignantly, "does not totter."

"You love him, don't you?"

Bertie drew herself up haughtily. "Didn't that finishing school I sent you to—at considerable cost, I may add—teach you that it's impolite to ask questions of such a personal nature?"

"It's never stopped *you*," C.J. reminded her darkly. "Out with it, Bertie—do you love him?"

Another sniff, a shrug, then a smile as coy and shy as any schoolgirl's. "I . . . like him, certainly."

"Uh-huh."

Bertie gave an impatient flounce. "Oh, all right, all right! Yes, I love the wretched man. I suppose you think that's disgusting. A woman my age being in love. Well, it is. I should know better. I *do* know better."

"I think it's wonderful," C.J. said with a soft laugh. "He adores you, you know. I just can't figure out why you didn't admit it years ago and end the suspense."

"We *thought* it was simple infatuation," Bertie replied in bemusement. "Year after year, we simply thought we'd come to our senses one day and that would be that. He *is* the butler, after all. One does not marry the butler without serious consideration, you know."

"Well, I think twenty-three years of serious consideration is about long enough, don't you? He's coming up to see you in a little while. And I want you to tell him you'll marry him."

"I'll think about it."

C.J. nodded, trying to figure out how—now that she'd worked the conversation around to weddings—she was going to tell Bertie that she and Garrett were married. She had to do it just right, letting Bertie think it had all been Garrett's idea and managing, somehow, to pretend that it was the most wonderful, amazing thing that could have happened to her.

What she *wanted* to do was burst into tears and fling herself into the arms that had cradled her during so many crises in her life. Things were hopelessly entangled now. Sharing a bed with Garrett last night, making love with him, had made the charade even more intolerable. Before, she'd almost managed to convince herself that she *didn't* love him, that it had just been mild infatuation. But now...now every time he looked at her, it drove the knife a little deeper into her heart. Being married to a man you didn't love was bad enough; being married to a man you did love—but who didn't love you back—was a nightmare.

"Bertie," she said quietly, "I have to tell you something."

"And there's something I have to tell you, C.J." Bertie was frowning, her expression pensive.

"But this is important. It's about—"

"Later, C.J. What I have to say can't wait. I've been lying here for the past four days thinking about it, feeling guiltier and guiltier, and I have to get it off my chest in case...well, in case these charlatan witch doctors in here manage to bump me off before I get out."

"Bertie, will you stop saying things like that."

"Sorry, dear." Bertie reached out and patted C.J.'s hand. "I know I scared you half to death the other day, keeling over like that. I should have told you I was having a problem with my heart, I see that now. Willerson said I should tell you, so if something happened it would be less of a shock, but of course I thought I knew best." She smiled ruefully, her fingers clasping C.J.'s with surprising strength.

"That's my problem, always thinking I know what's best for everyone. I know I've been a terrible substitute mother to you over the years, bullying you and—"

"Terrible? Are you crazy? You've been a fabulous mother!"

"You're very sweet, but you're an abominable liar, child. I did the best I could, and most of the time it was pretty good. You ate well, you didn't go naked, you had a roof over your head. But I often think you couldn't have had a very happy childhood, locked away on an island with a bunch of crazy old people.''

"Bertie, I was in heaven. Sure, I learned to play poker when I was nine, and could swear like a sailor at ten, and had drunk hard liquor and smoked part of a cigar by the time I was twelve. But listening to you and your cronies argue about politics and literature and art and philosophy...my God, I got an education most people would kill for, and got it painlessly.''

Bertie smiled dryly. "Better hear me out before you start singing my praises too highly, dear. I have a confession to make.''

C.J.'s stomach knotted. "Oh?"

"I made a deal with Garrett Jameison that if he married you, I'd give him control of my share of Parsons Industrial,'' she said all in a rush, holding up her hand to stop C.J. from saying anything. "I know it was wrong, but I was terrified, C.J. I didn't...oh, heaven forgive me, I didn't think you could handle being all on your own. And I was worried about PI. It never occurred to me that you were interested in the business. And I never realized until these past few days just how competent you are. Hearing you talk about how you're taking care of things while I'm in here, the plans you have, the decisions you've made—I should have put you in to take Emmett Royce's place, I can see that now. You've grown up into a fine young businesswoman, C.J., and I've never even noticed. And I...oh, I just hope you can forgive me!''

"I think I should tell you something, Bertie.''

"In a minute, dear. I have to get this off my conscience once and for all. Arranging to have you marry a man who doesn't love you was the cruelest thing I could have done! It would have ruined your life, C.J.—no, don't interrupt! I know you're quite smitten with the man, as well you should be. But it was all an act with him, child. I *hired* him to sweep you off your feet, do you see? But I can't bear the thought of going to my grave knowing I'd forced you into a loveless marriage!''

C.J. felt the room start to spin and she sat down with a thump, blinking owlishly at Bertie. "What?"

"I know, I know—I was a wicked old woman to have meddled like that. But believe me—marrying Garrett Jameison is the *last* thing I want you to do! I'd never be able to forgive myself. You'll find a nice man who loves you and you'll be as happy as a goat in clover... but you see why I had to tell you as quickly as I could. I was terrified that while I was in here he'd make good on the deal and marry you before I could stop it."

"Oh... boy." C.J. took a deep breath, let it out again slowly. The room had stopped spinning, but it was closing in on her now, squeezing her, making it hard to breathe. "Oh, boy..."

"You're as white as a ghost, C.J.—I'm so sorry! Please forgive me. I didn't do it to hurt you, I just wanted—"

"No more, please." C.J. threw her hand up like a cop directing traffic. "I don't believe this. I just don't believe it...."

"I know you're furious with me, C.J. I'll tell Garrett our deal is off as soon as possible, of course."

"Of course," C.J. echoed numbly. She felt as though she'd stepped off a very high cliff and hadn't hit bottom yet, her mind still scrambling around trying to make sense of it all. Garrett, she found herself thinking... how in heaven's name could she tell Garrett about this latest twist? The whole thing was turning into a farcical romantic comedy worthy of Grant and Hepburn at their manic best!

Except, she reminded herself numbly, he hadn't wanted to get married in the first place. So this would probably suit him just fine. She could release him from a marriage he didn't want any part of, and no one would be any the wiser.

"Now, dear, what was it you wanted to tell me?"

"I, um, oh, it was nothing important, Bertie. I've forgotten now. I, uh, just remembered an important phone call I have to make. Why don't you have a nap now, and I'll be back in an hour and we can talk as long as you like, all right?"

Garrett was padding around the kitchen trying to decide what he wanted to eat when he heard C.J. come in. He poked at a banana of dubious vintage, decided to pass and pulled the fridge open. "How about Chinese tonight?" he called over his shoulder. "My meeting fell through, so we can just stay home and—"

"I have to talk to you."

There was something in C.J.'s voice that made Garrett look around, and when he saw the expression on her face he closed the fridge slowly, the muscles in the pit of his stomach pulling tight. "What is it? Is Bertie all right?"

"You have to call that judge again—the one who married us." She looked pale and distracted, a worried frown pulling her brows together. "We have to get an annulment, Garrett. As soon as possible. Before Bertie finds out what we've done."

It caught him so by surprise that he simply stared at her, certain he'd heard wrong. He'd *had* to have heard wrong, because—

"It has to be an annulment and not a divorce because she can never know. Technically we shouldn't even *be* married—so an annulment is just a . . . another technicality."

Again, he heard the word without really comprehending it. "Are you nuts?" he asked with a hint of laughter in his voice. "We're as married as it gets, Slick. I know we didn't have a big church wedding, and I know what ceremony we did have was over practically before it started—but we *are* married. Legally married. And it was, if you'll recall, pretty satisfactorily consummated.''

"No!" She started pacing. "I mean, yes, I know all that! But she doesn't want us to be married, Garrett. She told me it was a mistake—that she made a mistake. She doesn't want me to marry you. So we *have* to get it annulled, don't you see?"

Garrett felt something cold walk down his spine. "No," he said with deliberate calm, "I don't."

She looked at him impatiently. "It's not that difficult, Garrett—we simply call your friend and have him unmarry us."

"Unmarry?" It would have been funny, he thought idly, if she hadn't been so serious. "Is this some kind of weird game with you or something? First I *have* to marry you, and three days later you want out? Uh-uh. I don't think so.''

"Garrett, *please!* I know it's crazy, but no crazier than the deal you made with Bertie in the first place." She combed her hair off her forehead with her hand, her small expressive face worried. "My God, I can't believe I actually went through with it. I don't know what I was thinking...even Bertie saw how insane the whole idea was."

She was talking more to herself than him, pacing the floor like a cat in a cage, and as he watched her, Garrett realized he'd gone cold and a little empty. She was right—it *had* been crazy. But they'd done it anyway, and now she wanted to—

"No one even has to know," she was saying. "The only people who know are Winthrup and the judge—and they won't tell Bertie."

"We know," Garrett heard himself saying in a low vibrant voice. "Damn it, C.J.—you and I know." He thought of last night with her, holding her, being part of her, feeling that ultimate closeness of two people joined by breath, by heartbeat, by soul.

She looked up at him, her face registering surprise. "But neither one of us even wanted it."

"So that means it doesn't count?" His voice rose slightly in spite of his best efforts. She was right—they *hadn't* wanted it. So why did the thought of getting free of a woman and a relationship he didn't want fill him with such anger?

"We made a mistake, Garrett. Both of us. But this is a chance to start over again, as though it never happened."

"Maybe we did make a mistake," he got out between gritted teeth, "but it *did* happen, C.J. And no amount of *unmarrying* is going to change what's happened." *What's happened between us,* he'd almost said, catching himself in time. But had it been between them, or had he been the only one feeling those things he'd started to feel?

She was looking at him oddly, the frown between her brows even deeper. "I don't understand why you're so angry," she said with a hint of impatience. "It was all just business to you, anyway. I thought you'd be *pleased*, for crying out loud!"

"Pleased? At being jerked around like a damned puppet on a string according to *your* whims?"

She did, he noticed, have the decency to look embarrassed. "I—I know it must seem like that. But honestly, Garrett, I'm only trying to do what's right for all of us. You don't love me—you've come out and said it to my face. And I married you because I thought it was what Bertie wanted, not because it was what *I* wanted. If we stay married, we're going to wind up making each other miserable."

He stared at her angrily, part of him wanting to tell her flat out that they were staying married and that was that—that he was tired of being shuffled around like a pawn on a chess board for *her* convenience, because of what *she* wanted. But another part of him, a cold, empty part, knew she was right. He'd once thought that Bertie's idea of a marriage of convenience had some merit, but he knew now that it was the worst of all worlds.

"If it'll make you happy," he finally said, quietly. There was a flicker of some dark emotion deep in her eyes, a look on her face that—for a split second—might have been utter desolation. But she turned away before he could be sure, head down, and nodded, saying nothing.

The emptiness gaped in him like a windswept canyon, bottomless, sear, dark. His throat felt constricted and his head had started to ache suddenly, the muscles across his shoulders and neck in knots. "I'll call Cartwright in the morning," he said in a clipped, hard voice. "And I'll spend the night in a hotel."

"You don't have to do that." She turned, her eyes glistening slightly, as though from unshed tears. "I'm flying across to Fort Myers in an hour—Bertie wants me to pick up some of her things from Paradise, and I've got to check the mail and ... and so on."

He nodded, his face feeling tight. "When will you be back?"

"Tomorrow afternoon, probably. I-I'll call and leave a message where I'll be staying."

"Fine." There didn't seem to be anything else to say. He stood there looking at her, wondering why he suddenly felt as though he was losing everything he had, everything he'd ever wanted. And how he'd ever managed to convince himself that no one would get hurt. "I'll have Cartwright draw up the necessary papers and call you when they're ready. I don't know what's involved. But it didn't take much to get us married." He smiled slightly, bitterly. "I doubt it'll take much to get us unmarried."

"Yeah." She nodded, blinking rapidly, and he wondered at the catch in her voice. "I, um, guess that's all, then."

All, he thought savagely. You come into my damned life and turn it upside down and then walk out again, and you say that's *all?* "Yeah, I guess so." He felt brittle and stiff, and he turned away and walked into the living room. "I'll be seeing you, C.J. Take care of yourself."

He poured himself a stiff shot of bourbon and stood at the windows and stared out across the restless Atlantic, filled with anger and resentment and an odd, undefined pain that seemed all-consuming. In the background, he could hear the click of her heels on hardwood as she walked through to the bedrooms, refused to turn and follow her. Instead, he stood by the windows until a few minutes later he heard the sound of her footsteps crossing to the door, the click of the lock, then a long pause—as though she was standing there looking at him, waiting for him to say something. Then the door quietly, finally, closed.

He finished the bourbon in one swallow, wincing as it burned its way down, and felt the silences of the room come stealing in from the corners, thick as shadows. For the short while that she'd been here, she'd filled these same rooms with laughter and vitality and music, and he'd become used to catching a hint of her perfume on the air or hearing her singing softly, or just looking around and catching sight of her, tucked into the contours of his world like someone who belonged there.

And suddenly, savagely, he wheeled around and threw the glass across the room with every ounce of strength he had. It hit the far wall and exploded into slivers of flying glass, and he stood there, breathing fast, fists clenched, the anger burning through him.

Then, just as suddenly, the fury vanished. In its wake came a deep, chilling loneliness that seemed to echo the stillness of the big empty rooms around him. He found himself listening carefully, hoping to catch some hint that she hadn't left at all. That in a moment or two she'd come out in a swirl of happy laughter and teasing looks and walk across and step into his arms.

But there was nothing. She was gone.

Jamie Kildonan, border lord, pirate, ne'er-do-well, gazed out of the canvas at C.J. accusingly, his dark brows pulled together, mouth hard with anger, looking as handsome and sullen and untamable as ever.

What in heaven's name did Chastity even *see* in him? He was arrogant and hostile and ferociously aggressive. He lacked finesse, delicacy, tenderness. He wanted everything his way, he demanded, he argued, he challenged everything she said or did or wanted. He took her to bed without promises, refusing to relinquish his precious independence, and when he was tired of her, he walked off without a backward glance until the next time. He didn't give her a damned thing besides aggravation and heartache, and yet she loved him. Without doubt, without reservation, with every bit of her being.

Men!

Mouth tight with anger, C.J. lifted the canvas from the easel and stalked across to the storage cupboard in her small Pullman kitchen. She was tired of him looking at her. Tired of the way his eyes kept following her, speculative, thoughtful, a little dangerous.

Pulling the cupboard door open, she shoved the canvas in behind a stack of storage boxes, face to the wall, then slammed the door closed.

It was echoed by a crash of thunder that made her flinch and she glanced at the big front window, seeing nothing but sheets of wind-driven rain and flickers of lightning. Water poured down the glass as though someone had turned a fire hose on it, and she shivered, wishing it would let up.

The storm had come roaring up out of the gulf like a juggernaut early that same morning, not close enough to hurricane force to deserve the dignity of a name, but severe enough to cause weather warnings up and down the coast.

The waves were crashing up on the beach like locomotives, huge and yellow with churned-up sand, spume flying from their ragged crests. Along the edge of the beach, the palms were being whipped back and forth like rag dolls, the occasional frond tearing free to go cartwheeling through the air.

A good day to stay inside and work.

Well, she was managing the first part all right—staying indoors. The rest of it, though, was a dead loss.

It would help if she could quit crying. But ever since she'd gotten back to Paradise, the tears just wouldn't stop.

It hurt, damn it! She'd done the absolute stupidest thing she could have done—fallen in love with him—and now she was paying for it in spades, her heart feeling as though it had been hit by a fleet of trucks.

As happened every time she thought about it, her eyes filled and she had to blink to keep from stumbling over the furniture. It had been so easy to let herself believe that— given time—he could learn to love her. She'd known better, of course. If there was one thing she'd learned, it was that common sense and love didn't have a damned thing to do with each other.

Wiping her cheeks with her sleeve, she took a deep breath and walked across to the closet she'd been trying to clean for the past two hours. She'd already scrubbed the floors and vacuumed the rugs and tidied and washed the kitchen cupboards. Yesterday she'd sorted all her books, by author and title, then had cataloged all her compact discs and her videotape collection. And tomorrow...tomorrow, if the weather cooperated, she was going to go to Fort Myers and have lunch in a nice restaurant and go shopping and buy something frivolous and then come home and bury herself in a good mystery, a glass or two of wine and a long, hot bubble bath.

The wind banged against the door and whined at the window, wanting in. Something moved in the sheets of blowing rain just beyond that window and she squinted at it, seeing a flicker of bright yellow. And then, with no warning, someone was standing there, hands cupped around his face, peering in at her.

Garrett Jameison. He spotted her at the same instant she realized who it was and she could see his mouth moving, as though he was trying to shout over the bellow of the wind as he gestured toward the door.

Open it, he seemed to be saying. *I want to talk to you.*

Heart somewhere in her throat, C.J. shook her head frantically and gestured for him to go away, praying he hadn't been able to see the tears on her cheeks. What on earth was he doing here!

There was a terrific pounding at the door and she stared at it, then marched across to it purposefully. "Go away! I'm busy!"

"C.J., for—" The rest of it was lost, torn away by the wind. "—talk to you, damn it! I'm drowning out here! Open the door!"

Great! Terrific! She was falling apart, looking like the victim of a shipwreck, hair stringy, eyes swollen from crying, cheeks puffy, and he had to choose *this* particular day to turn up again. He'd take one look at her and know exactly what was wrong. He'd told her not to fall in love with him. That if she did, she'd only be hurt. And here she was, living proof that he'd been right.

Well, she was damned if she was going to give him the satisfaction of being able to say he'd told her so. "I said I'm busy," she shouted through the door. "Go up to the house—I'll come up later." When she'd had time to collect some of her composure, put on a little makeup and just generally haul herself back together.

There was a responding mutter that sounded more profane than agreeable, then silence. Holding her breath, she stood there uncertainly for another minute or two, then let the breath out in a sigh of relief.

He wasn't here to see her, anyway. No doubt he was just clearing his things out of his makeshift office. Tying up a few loose ends. Bertie had come home yesterday and he probably had things to discuss with her, especially now that his deal with her had fallen through. Bertie had hoped she'd be able to convince him to stay on and help her with PI, but C.J. doubted that was going to happen. Sitting on the board of someone else's corporation was not Garrett Jameison's style. The only reason he'd agreed to do it in the first place was because of . . . her.

She swallowed and blinked back another treacherous spill of tears, wondering how long it was going to take for her to realize how lucky she was to have gotten out unscathed. Had they stayed married, her life would have turned into a living hell, having to pretend she felt nothing for him while sleeping in his bed, making love with him, having his children. . . .

Something hit the door with a crash that made the window shudder and C.J. jumped, wondering if the trellis had blown over, bougainvillea and all. She contemplated having a quick look at the damage, but before she could even move there was another resounding crash and in the next instant the door had flown open in an explosion of lashing rain and wind.

A tall, broad-shouldered figure in a yellow slicker strode in out of the storm, pausing long enough to push the door closed against the wind and jam it with his shoulder. Garrett turned and threw the hood back, rainwater pouring off him. Then he shook his head, spraying water like a wet dog, before pulling the slicker off and dropping it in a heap. "I want to talk to you."

C.J. stepped back reflexively, breath catching a little as he loomed toward her. And she had a fleeting thought that he looked large and dangerous, exactly like Jamie had in *Sweet Secrets* when he'd chased Chastity into the old walled city and had hunted her like a wolf a rabbit, finally trapping her in the old abbey. He'd come crashing through the door just as Garrett had done, tall and fierce, eyes burning....

"What do you want?" Her voice ended in a squeak and she swallowed, reminding herself that this wasn't Jamie Kildonan, but Garrett Jameison. Somehow not finding that truth even half as reassuring as it should have been. "You can't just break down my door and—"

"I want you."

"I—" She stared at him, mouth half-open. "Excuse me?"

"I said I want you." He looked grim and determined, and C.J. took another step backward. "You're mine, damn it— legal as hell. And I'm not giving you up. Not without a fight." He was on her in two long strides and before she could do more than recoil, he'd grabbed her shoulders with his hands and had pulled her toward him. And then his mouth was on hers, slick and cold and sweet with rain, and he was kissing her fiercely.

He released her after a moment and C.J. stumbled back, trying to catch her breath.

"I know you don't love me, but I've never given you a chance. We've never given each *other* a chance." He grinned suddenly, the lamplight glistening on his rain-wet face. "Hell, even Chastity gave Jamie a chance, C.J. That's all I want. I'll give you the annulment if you really want it—but at least give it a try first. At least give yourself a *chance* to love me."

"But I do," she said in a small voice, feeling a little dazed. If it weren't for the wind screaming around the splintered wood of her front door, she'd have sworn she was dreaming.

"I know this is a crazy way to—" He stopped dead. Blinked. Frowned a little. "You do?"

"Of course."

"But...I...you..." He swore softly, scooping a handful of dripping hair off his forehead. "You never told me that."

"You made me promise not to."

"Well, hell," he growled, "since when did you ever pay any attention to anything I said?"

"You were *very* emphatic about it. You told me clearly that I was *not,* under any circumstances, to fall in love with you."

"I obviously didn't know what the hell I was talking about."

Her mouth curved with a smile. "I see. Does that mean I shouldn't believe *anything* you tell me?"

"No." His own smile widened and his eyes captured hers, warm with memories. "There are a few things I can tell you that you can believe. That when I'm with you I feel like a kid again, and when I'm not with you I'm miserable. That I haven't done a damned day's work since you left because I can't keep my mind on anything but figuring out how to get you back. That I can't close my eyes without seeing you, or go to bed without dreaming of you, or see a woman on the street without wishing it were you.

"That the only thing I want in the whole damn world is to wake up every morning for the rest of my life and see you lying beside me. That I want to make love to you and make kids with you and have a life with you. Those are a *few* of the things you can by God believe."

"Oh." She drew in an unsteady breath. "That covers about everything, I should think."

"Not quite." His lips curved up in a lazy, wolfish grin that made her toes curl slightly. "I could also tell you that making love with you is like nothing I've experienced before. That when you're all wrapped around me it's like I've found a part of myself I never even knew was missing and I can't breathe properly and everything gets fuzzy and confused."

Then his expression grew suddenly serious, and he held her gaze steadily. "And that you scare the hell out of me, C.J. I always thought that feeling like this about a woman meant nothing but trouble. When I agreed to Bertie's deal, I did it because I figured I was safe, that I'd never start to...care. And then this past month I tried to convince myself that I'd be smarter to just let you go. But I can't. I'm in too deep. I just don't want to lose you, C.J., it's that simple."

"Oh," she said again, knowing it was scarcely adequate but too dazed to think of anything more clever. "I, um, are you saying that you want to stay married?"

"Only forever, C.J.," he murmured, coming across and cupping her face in his hands. He gazed down at her, those tawny-gold eyes fierce. "I want you. I want to be your husband. Not as part of some deal to make Bertie happy, but because I—" He frowned and she could see him struggling with it, trying to say it, the words so unfamiliar and alien to him that they lodged in his throat. "I need you," he whispered. "Don't send me away, C.J. At least give me a chance."

"I love you," she replied quite simply, reaching up to touch his rain-wet cheek.

"You're not just saying that?" He looked a little worried. "I mean, I hoped you would. Eventually, anyway. But I figured all those things you said were just...part of the role you were playing. You said you were trying to make it easy for me."

"Not that easy," she said with a soft laugh. "And the only time I lied to you was when I said I didn't love you."

"Do you think Bertie knew this was going to happen?"

"I wouldn't doubt it for a minute."

"She was right about Dad and Krystal." He winced slightly. "And so were you. She really does love him. And I think it's going to last this time. I think it's for real."

"Have you talked to your dad?"

"They're in Lauderdale visiting friends, and I flew up yesterday. Dad was pretty cool and things got kind of tense until I explained why I was there, but in the end it was Krystal who smoothed things over." He grinned suddenly, giving his head a shake. "She's one hell of a lady. Dad's a lucky guy to have found her. And I guess, in a way, I am, too. It was seeing them together that made me realize that if I didn't come after you, I was throwing away the chance of a lifetime. It's not enough to have happiness just fall into your lap—you've got to have brains enough to recognize it. And the guts to grab it when it does."

"And does that mean you're grabbing me, Sir Jameison?"

"With both hands," he growled, slipping his arms tightly around her.

"That," she murmured with a teasing smile, "sounds as though it just might have possibilities." Her fingers strayed to the top button of his shirt and she toyed with it, looking up through her lashes at him. "One of a wife's duties is to see to her husband's comfort, and you can't be very comfortable in these sopping-wet clothes."

His eyes narrowed slightly, burning with a dangerous hunger that sent a little shiver darting through her. "If we're going to discuss wifely duties, I can think of another one that would do a hell of a lot for my comfort right now."

"Really?" She looked up at him in wide-eyed innocence. "And what would that be?"

"Come here and I'll tell you," he murmured, lowering his mouth to her ear and doing just that.

"Oh." It was no more than a breathless gasp and C.J. had to cling to the front of his shirt to keep her knees from buckling. "You mean right . . . now?"

"Why not?" he replied quite practically, dropping his hands to the row of buttons marching down the front of her cotton blouse and starting to slip them free. "It shouldn't take more than a couple of hours."

And later, loving him, filled with him, desire became a white-hot trembling fire within her, drawing tighter and tighter until she had to cry out with the wonder of it. Twisting, moving, legs tight around him, she tried to call his name but managed only an urgent moan instead, and then she was panting against his mouth, whispering wordless things filled with her need, her love.

And then he was moving in that way he had, strong and swift and sure, right to the melting core of her, and she heard a soaring cry of joy break through the lamplit shadows of the room and realized it was her own voice as it filled her, shattered, filled her again, washing through her in a long, silken wave.

She half heard Garrett's harsh groan and the rasp of his breathing against her throat, felt the muscles in his back knot and buck and then his voice, thick, tortured, "C.J. . . . C.J. . . . C.J. . . . ."

She tried to answer him but couldn't, too breathless from the flash fire of raw sensation pouring through her to do more than moan again, softly, as he sagged, shuddering, into her arms.

It seemed like an eternity later that Garrett realized he was still lying full-length between C.J.'s slender thighs, locked in her arms and the sweet prison of her body. He lifted onto his forearms and smiled drowsily. "I could roll over onto the other side of the bed," he murmured, "or just stay here until I've caught my breath."

She smiled back, a lazy, satisfied smile like a cat still savouring stolen cream. Stretching languorously, she wrapped her legs across the backs of his. "Stay. Unless it's going to take till morning."

"Keep moving around like that and I can guarantee it won't take that long."

"I love you, Garrett." Slipping her arms around him, she kissed his chest, then took a tuft of hair between her teeth and tugged it gently. "Am I allowed to say that now?"

"Often," he growled, lowering his mouth to hers and kissing her playfully. "And I, um . . ."

"I know."

"It shouldn't be so hard to say."

"Yes, it should. If it means anything, it should be the hardest thing in the world to say."

"It does. And it is." He grinned, then sighed. "C.J., I do love you." The words weren't, surprisingly, even half as difficult to get out as he'd expected. He thought about that for a moment, then tried again, almost experimentally. "I love you. I *love* you. I love *you*. Damn!" He laughed out loud, gazing down at her in wonderment. "This is easy. I love you."

He said it a time or two more just as practice, liking the way the words felt on his tongue. Liking the sound of them. Liking the look they ignited in C.J.'s soft eyes. Impossibly, he felt himself respond to both words and look, stirring slightly—but unmistakably—within the hot silk of her body.

He moved gently, pressing himself into her more deeply. "Too soon to really mean anything," he whispered, seeing her eyes widen slightly, watching her catch her lower lip between her teeth. He moved again, taunting himself with what wasn't—yet—possible, smiling as he felt her tighten around him, felt the almost imperceptible shift of her hips, the tautening of muscle, the slippery blossom of heat.

"I couldn't possibly," she said in a half moan. "Not so soon. Not yet. I couldn't—we can't..."

And yet, in less time than Garrett would have thought possible, they were. C.J. was whispering his name over and over, voice all but lost under the silken glissade of slippery flesh on flesh and his own soft catch of breath every time he pressed himself into the heat of her.

Time vanished, folding in on itself and becoming meaningless, as meaningless as everything in the world but the warm, alive woman moving urgently in his arms, and then it was coming together like the crash of storm-driven breakers and he was consumed by it, losing himself gladly, joyously...

And thinking in that split second of ultimate clarity before the last blinding uprush that love was, after all, the simplest thing in the world.

* * * * *

**Silhouette Books
is proud to present
our best authors,
their best books...
and the best in
your reading pleasure!**

Throughout 1993, look for exciting books
by these top names in contemporary
romance:

CATHERINE COULTER—
Aftershocks in February

FERN MICHAELS—
Nightstar in March

DIANA PALMER—
Heather's Song in March

ELIZABETH LOWELL
Love Song for a Raven in April

SANDRA BROWN
(previously published under
the pseudonym Erin St. Claire)—
Led Astray in April

LINDA HOWARD—
All That Glitters in May

When it comes to passion,
we wrote the book.

Silhouette®

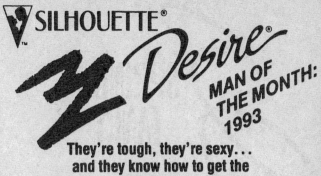

SILHOUETTE® Desire®

HAWK'S WAY

HAWK'S WAY—where the Whitelaws of Texas run free till passion brands their hearts. A hot new series from Joan Johnston!

Look for the first of a long line of Texan adventures, beginning in April with THE RANCHER AND THE RUNAWAY BRIDE (D #779), as Tate Whitelaw battles her bossy brothers—and a sexy rancher.

Next, in May, Faron Whitelaw meets his match in THE COWBOY AND THE PRINCESS (D #785).

Finally, in June, Garth Whitelaw shows you just how hot the summer can get in THE WRANGLER AND THE RICH GIRL (D #791).

Join the Whitelaws as they saunter about HAWK'S WAY looking for their perfect mates . . . only from Silhouette Desire!